They Drive By Night

They Drive
By Night
James Curtis

With an introduction by Jonathan Meades

LONDON BOOKS CLASSICS

LONDON BOOKS
PO Box 52849
London SW11 1SE
www.london-books.co.uk

First published 1938 by Jonathan Cape
This edition published by London Books 2008

The publisher wishes to thank Nicolette Edwards
for supplying information used in the production of this book

A catalogue record for this book
is available from the British Library

ISBN 978-0-9551851-4-4

Printed and bound in Great Britain by
CPI Antony Rowe

Typeset by Octavo Smith Ltd in Plantin 10.5/13.5
www.octavosmith.com

INTRODUCTION

James Curtis (1907–1977) and Robin Cook (1931–1994) were both brought up in keenly philistine families whose bourgeois mores they eschewed in favour of orthodoxly intemperate bohemianism, borderline criminality and lowlife. They both attended public schools which, conventionally enough, they hated: Curtis, The King's School, Canterbury; Cook, Eton College. They both changed their name. Geoffrey Maiden became James Curtis, not least because Maiden was a laughably prim name to adorn the cover of the sort of books he would write. Cook became Derek Raymond because, by the time he started writing again in the early 1980s after more than a decade's hiatus, there was an airport hack of the same name.

In Eric Partridge's opinion these were the two novelists who, during his long lexicographical career, were the most abundant sources of English slang. Indeed Partridge did as much as anyone to save them from oblivion and should be honoured for doing so. Though it has to be said that there is an element of mutual dependence: his debt to Curtis is immense. Without him he would have had little knowledge of what was pejoratively styled the 'unconventional usage' of the era when he began collating: slang, like sex, had always been with us but in mid-C20 England neither were fictively portrayed with any degree of candour. As his sceptical and more rigorous successor Jonathon Green has observed, Partridge's 'lexicographical method was less than wholly scrupulous . . . his etymologizing sometimes tendentious'. To which it must be added that Partridge was often gullible. He failed to acknowledge that novelists *invent.* They invent themselves, they invent character, milieu, place, incident and, likely as not, coinages. This is – or ought to be – obvious in the case of an artist as exhibitionistically baroque as Cook, who tended to cagey amnesia when discussing his argotic sources. James Curtis was a quieter writer. But he was not a reporter even if he relies on exaggeratedly naturalistic observation. His fiction is just that – fiction. His artifice is of a sort which dissembles itself. Green's database for his *Cassell's Dictionary Of Slang* and *Green's Dictionary Of Slang On Historical Principles* includes more than a thousand citations from Curtis, among them three hundred from *They Drive By Night* alone. He is inclined to believe that Curtis's vernacular is genuinely representational of small-time criminals of the 1930s. Still, every slang word, like every folk song, comes from somewhere. It always has an author: the simile operative, the rhymer, usually the show-off. The idea that slang is a covert and excluding code is wide of the mark. It is flashier than that. We should bear in mind the way that criminals proudly flaunt their criminality – their houses, their clothes, their jewels, their molls, their 'cherished' numberplates granted them by Cecil Parkinson. Slang is akin. It may belong to cadres and castes but it is as exhibitionistic as a tattoo. It is low-fi verbal invention, the poetry of gutter and tronk, the poetry of poetry-despisers. And it was itself despised in Curtis's England by usage tyrants who failed to acknowledge that its richness dignified the work of Shakespeare, Vanbrugh, Sterne, Dickens and, especially, Joyce. The linguistic straits of the time are drearily advertised in the old maid's prose of the majority of green Penguins. Curtis was in orange Penguin. His language is vital and often very funny: galloping your antelope (masturbation); toby (high road); pen (stink); ackermaracker (tea); the sweeny (flying squad, forty years before Waterman and Thaw); stone ginger (a racing certainty, a term he also uses).

The proposition that *there are no genres, only talents*, is particularly appropriate in the case of James Curtis. His work is sui generis. It belongs to no particular tradition. He appears to have a comprehensive knowledge of the society he is writing about. Again, this is not to imply that his method is documentary even if it pretends to be. Rather, that he convinces with specific detail which is not necessarily 'real'; but there is so much of it and it is so precisely limned that he persuades his reader that this is how it is. There is no hint of the wishful pseudo-American fantasy that infects so much British (and French) hard-boiled fiction of the era. Curtis did not write thrillers or mysteries. Nor does he possess any but the most tangential affinity to the vaguely proletcultist former miners, stokers and construction workers whose didactic slices of dignified working-class life were a novelistic staple of the interbellum. Equally he is not a social anthropologist, a worker for Mass Observation, though he evidently shares some of that movement's pre-occupations.

His novels are literary constructions whose characters would be unlikely to read them. These characters – minor crims, prostitutes, spivs, coppers, lorry drivers, waitresses – tend to helplessness. They are largely incapable of resolving their lives. They are as much victims of inexorable fate as, say, Theseus and Phaedra. But fate here is social and economic. Like many middle-class writers of the 1930s, Curtis was in thrall to Marxism and his people are, broadly, creatures of cultural determinism, bereft of choice, inured to poverty and to scraping along, hardly daring to dream of social ascent, blindly pursuing mapped routes which they are powerless to amend: they drift because they have no choice. In *They Drive By Night* Curtis leaves his readers to discern this for themselves.

Published in 1938 it was Curtis's fourth novel in less than three years. The protagonist Shorty Mathews bears a resemblance to William Kennedy, the titular character of

The Gilt Kid, Curtis's debut. The slang and the seediness of the settings are also kindred. But the techniques are different. This is an altogether harsher work. Curtis relies here on understatement and suggestion. He eschews an editorial voice and espouses a moral neutrality. He seldom comments on the characters. He neither sits in judgment nor grants his personae sentimental nobility. There is a sort of authorial absence. The book is speedy, elliptical. Much of the action is carried by terse, phonetically reported speech which may today seem corny to start with – but persist, for it becomes compelling and attests to the degree to which rhythms and patterns are as generationally determined as locutions. *They Drive By Night*'s construction – like that of, say, Waugh's *Vile Bodies* or Greene's early entertainments, but unlike that of *The Gilt Kid* – is obviously indebted to cinematic montage. Curtis didn't write what Anthony Burgess (astonishingly only ten years his junior) sarcastically deprecated as Class A fiction – work that has no literary merit and only comes to life when it is filmed. Nonetheless Curtis certainly wrote with an eye to adaptation, and *They Drive By Night* was duly filmed within months of its publication. Curtis co-wrote the screenplay and the director was Arthur Woods. A notably creepy Ernest Thesiger was cast as Hoover and the loudmouthed music-hall comedian Ronald Shiner was Charley. Emlyn Williams, then at the height of his stardom following *Night Must Fall,* played Shorty. He was 33 and probably ten years too old for the role. Curtis's characters are hardly out of their teens. Their youth is one of their essential components, one of the causes of their poignancy, vulnerability, unworldliness and hopelessness. They are absolute beginners *avant la lettre*.

The world they inhabit is hermetic: it is grimy, shabby, threadbare, tired. Curtis is a master of squalid décor. Page upon page reeks of coal gas and swill, soot and smuts, bleach and carbolic, drains and lard, Woodbines and belching tea-urns. His descriptions of the reeking cafés frequented by prostitutes and ponces recall his contemporary Edward Burra's rare London canvasses, works of distortion and hyperbole. Curtis was an artist of the same sensibility who conjured a low-key exoticism out of drabness. His plots may lack drama, but no matter – they are sufficient armature on which to hang a singular portrait of a milieu which may or may not have been of his own invention. Even he probably didn't know.

Jonathan Meades

CHAPTER I

Gradually it grew lighter. Men in wide sombreros and thigh boots were washing the streets. Bums on the benches in Trafalgar Square shivered uneasily beneath the rough caress of the dawn breeze blowing up Whitehall; soon the parks would open. In the all-night café bars the waiters nipped their cigarettes and began to sweep the floor, for most of the night birds had gone home and now the places would gradually fill up with people on their way to work. Milkmen clattered by. The last whores went home, some by taxi cab to Maida Vale, some by all-night tram to Kennington. In Covent Garden, Spitalfields, Billingsgate, the Borough Market, Smithfield, work was well under way.

Lorries, drays and coal carts were clattering down the Caledonian Road. Trams were growing more frequent and the first buses had started. An unshaven man climbed to the top deck of a tram and lighted his pipe. The tram jolted and he had not yet got a paper to read. When the conductor came to take his fare he spoke.

'Penny please, mate.'

The conductor, swaying, punched the ticket. The man felt lonely in the dawn and spoke again.

'Going to be a nice morning.'

The conductor grunted.

'Going to be all right for some,' he grudged. 'What about that poor bastard there. Last morning he's ever going to see.'

He jerked his thumb in the direction of Pentonville Prison, which the tram was just passing.

'Yerce. That's right. Allen. They're hanging him this morning, ain't they?'

'Blimey, I wonder how he slept.'

'Not bleeding much, I reckon.'

The conductor went downstairs.

If Allen was sleepless he was not the only man in the prison who was awake. Pacing up and down his cell, leaning his head against the lime-washed bricks, watching the dawn help the bars to make a changing pattern on his cell floor was another prisoner. He ran his hand over his stubbly chin and sat for a moment on the table ledge fixed into an angle of the wall.

His name was Albert Mathews, the boys all called him Shorty, and outside his cell hung a notice saying:

CARDS AT OFFICE

His cards were at the office because he was being discharged that morning, going out into the world where men didn't sleep under the same roof as people who were going to be strangled at a set hour.

Glancing at the rumpled heap of blankets that lay on his bed boards he sighed.

Well, that was the end of that. No more sleeping on wooden planks, no more bed bugs, as much lavatory paper as he wanted. A twenty-one month sentence over. Twenty-one moon was five hundred and thirty-six nights in stir if you kept your nose clean and got your full remission, five hundred and forty-three if you went and lost seven days like a berk.

He'd been lucky and all if you looked at it that way. Blimey, with the record he'd got he'd 've been entitled to draw a lagging or five stretch. It was next stop Parkhurst for a racing certainty. The Scrubs, Wandsworth and twice in the Ville. Keep it up, boy. You'll spend the end of your life doing a nice little piece of Preventive Detention in Portsmouth. Good old Pompey. That's where all the right herbs ended up. Pompey or being topped like that poor bastard Allen.

Topping one bloke and letting another out to have a little run. That's the way it came. One thing about this bloke Allen. He was a punk. He wasn't stir-wise. They always seemed to be topping geezers who'd never seen the inside of a nick before. Well, maybe it came easier that way. Maybe it didn't. If you'd never done a bit of bird you didn't know what it was like when they topped a guy. Well, all ways up, it must be a bastard spending the last three weeks of your life locked up and being monotonously eaten to death by the Ville bed bugs. Gawd, a bloke must want to sleep in a clean bed just once more before he died.

Shorty got out and mechanically squashed a bug that was running across the floor. It left a red stain on the boards. The next bloke who lived in the cell would have to scrub that out. You weren't supposed to squash bugs on the floor. When your three planks got more than usually cooty you were supposed to write 'bugs' on them with chalk and leave them outside the cell door. Next day you got them back. They were just as cooty as ever.

He strolled up and down again. It was getting quite light now. The time must be somewhere round about six o'clock. Allen had got about another three hours. When Shorty was having a pint in a pub, Allen's body would just about be burned up with quick-lime. First they topped you, then they poured water on you, then they burnt you.

Blimey, he'd like to get out of this cell. This was the third bloke they'd topped while he'd been in the Ville this time. The screws ought to be around soon letting the blokes out of their floweries. Come on, blimey, make it a bit sharpish . . .

*

At St Albans a lorry driver was sitting hunched up at the counter of a transport café. He drained the last drop out of his thick tea-cup and sucked his teeth appreciatively. The man behind the counter yawned and scratched his head. The lorry driver lit the cigarette end that he'd been keeping behind his ear.

'Going to the Smoke?' yawned the counterman.

The driver nodded.

'Be back here tonight, chum. Least I hope so. I'd like to get home tomorrow night. The missus is having a birthday.'

The counterman laughed.

'You and your missus,' he said. 'What you transport blokes want to get married for I don't know. Stone me if I do. Anybody'd think there wasn't no girls on the road.'

'Gi' us another tea.'

He pushed his cup along the counter and glanced towards the doorway. It had suddenly been darkened by the figure of a man.

'What-ho, Alf.'

'How you going on, me old Charley?'

'Mustn't grumble, mate. Mustn't grumble. Tea please and a bacon sandwich.'

The newcomer went over and stuck a penny into the slide of a pin-table machine.

'Nice weather for this time o' the year,' said the counterman as he poured out the two cups of tea, exaggerating the smartness with which he manipulated the tea pot.

'Yerce?' Alf took a last drag out of his cigarette and threw it on the floor to make one more burn in the linoleum. 'Think so? You want to try a bit of bleeding driving these nights when there ain't no moon. You'd know all right whether it was nice weather or not, wouldn't he, Charley?'

'Do what, mate? Gaw damn. You bleeding made me go and miss it.'

'Whyn't you leave that board alone and buy yourself

some fags? Acting bloody silly, that's what you're doing. Bloody mug to yourself, that's what you are.'

'All right, all right. Ain't nothing to do with you is it?'

'Ain't nothing to do with me? 'Ark at her. Blimey, I like that. That's a right stroke to come out with. Drawn your wages and all yesterday, tomorrow up at Coventry you'll be trying to ponce a cup of tea off of me.'

'Gawd stone me blind. I bin and missed it again. If you'd only leave me alone I'd know what I was doing of. Nothing but chat all the time.'

Alf jerked a thumb towards Charley.

''Ark at her carrying on. You'd think he was bleeding good or something the way he talks. Got 'smorning's?'

A newspaper boy with a cap over one eye and a dripping nose had just come in.

'Here y'are, mister. 'Spress. One penny.'

'You'll get some bleeding nooks. Let's have a look at it.'

He took a paper and spread it out on the counter, looking at it with the widened eyes more accustomed to the open road than to printed pages.

''Anging him this morning they are and all.'

'Who? Allen?' The counterman was lifting up the empty cups.

'Yerce.' Alf was feeling in his pocket for another cigarette end.

'Had it coming to him and all he did, the way he done that tart in. Some blokes ain't safe to be around.'

'That's right, mate.' Alf sucked his teeth. He had no more dog ends in his pocket.

Charley looked up from the pin-table into which he had just fed his fifth penny.

'You wait till some old dear gets on your nerves mate, then you'll sing a different tune I shouldn't wonder.'

The counterman jerked a thumb.

'Trust old Charley. Allus got some bleeding moan.'

CHAPTER II

Shorty walked down the street. Trousers flapped easily around his legs. It felt a bit different from stir clobber. One thing nowadays they let you wear your own shoes the last week so you didn't have that light feeling in your feet like you used to years ago. Funny thing though, all the time you did you felt the same coming out. The Ville, where it was, was a bastard. You looked out of your window and saw the trams lumbering down the road. Lucky sons of bitches riding in trams and then you came out and it was all different. The bloody trams scared the life out of you. Well, Allen had kicked off now. And there he dangles on the tree, the soul of love and bravery, oh that such men should victims be of law and law's vile knavery. The best thing was to go in and buy a packet of fags. When you'd been in a gaff and bought yourself something and someone took your dough and spoke a bit civil to you life was a lot different.

He stepped into a cigarette shop. There was a smashing piece behind the counter. Her eyes looked kind of tired. Shorty looked at them and then looked away again. Thoughts were running through his mind. Judies like her had a good time. Blokes took them around and they didn't take them around for nothing. Proper game it was. Each knew what the other was after. It was just a case of how soon you flashed the old joy-stick. She smiled at him. It was the first girl who had smiled at him for eighty weeks.

'Large Player, please Miss.'

He planked down a shilling on the counter instead of the fourpence he had originally intended to pay for

Weights. A bloke had to buy tanner fags when there was a bride like this around. Smiling, she picked up his coin. Still smiling, she handed him his cigarettes and his ha'penny change. He hung around. It would be nice to chat this tart. It would be nice to be able to talk to her the way other blokes talked. His mouth was dry. What the hell could he say anyway? Right dopey bastard he was with a lovely bit like this and he didn't know how to set about it. Some blokes were too dopey to know how to cut themselves up a good dinner.

With trembling fingers he stripped the cellophane wrapper off the cigarette packet. His fingers were still shaking when he stuck the cigarette in his mouth. Matches. That was something to talk about.

'Box of red tips, Miss.'

She crinkled up her little nose in perplexity. Shorty felt his knees turn to water. He had forgotten what a tart could do to a bloke. Red tips. That was a stroke to be coming out with. As if a decent straight tart like her would know a word of that sort.

'Box of Swan's, I mean.'

She handed him his red-tipped matches. Their fingers touched. Shorty's hands trembled more than ever. He knew the pusher was laughing at him. Fumbling in his pocket he found the unaccustomed coins and tried to hand her over three-ha'pence. The ha'penny fell among the newspapers. Feeling a fool, Shorty tried to pick it up.

He moved a paper. It was an early racing edition, but it carried a headline of ordinary news. He glanced at it.

ALLEN HANGED: GAOL GATE SCENES

'Thank you, Miss. Good morning, Miss.'

He was out of the shop. He was walking down the street. He was striking a match on a lamppost. He was puffing at his lighted cigarette. It was no good. It was no good. She was one side of the fence, he was the other.

As happy as a prisoner just out of gaol. That's what they said. Who said? The mugs who didn't know what they were talking about. As happy as what? Go on mate, laugh that one off.

Plod. Plod. Plod. The pavements slipped away in the distance. The road curved uphill towards the stir and the trams came past. Trams. They were doing away with trams. Putting trolley buses on the road. Every time you came out of stir, something was different, something that made the world a little harder to live in.

He stood by King's Cross station wondering what to do next.

The whole day lay in front of him. The whole day and the next and the next and the next until he got himself knocked off again. He didn't want to do that. Hell of a long time the next bit of bird was going to be unless he got done for suspect. If a bloke got done for suspect he only got three months. Anybody could do a carpet. A bloke on exercise had said to him:

'You ain't half wide, mate. You don't know nothing. Take me. Fourteen cons I got and the longest sentence I ever served was a carpet. As soon as things start getting a bit hot I take a walk near a car park and get done for suspect. Blimey, I'm entitled to be doing a lagging now. Five stretch I'd of got if I had my rights. There's blokes in here doing too long and there's blokes ain't doing long enough. I'm one of the last. Suspected person. That's me. You can't beat it.'

What he'd like now would be to see a tart in bed. That'd be a bit of all right. Just to walk into a room and see her in bed. Blimey, what a slice of cake. That poor bastard Allen wasn't never going to see a tart in bed again. The quicklime was burning him up now. No more of the old Sir

Berkeley for him. Must make a bloke think a bit the last night he was going to be on earth. Plenty of time for thinking in the last twenty-four hours, and a couple of screws sitting and watching you all the time. The last human being who was going to touch you was the hangman. No more judy's arms round your neck, but the hangman fixing the rope.

He nipped his cigarette and stuck it behind his ear. The wind made his trousers flap. His legs were not used to being wrapped in loose trousers. Unaccustomed to pockets he held his hands loosely clasped behind his back and watched the trams clang round the corner. The hooves of the patient horses drawing the coal carts rang on the road. There was a faintly sour taste inside his stomach.

Go into a decent café and have a proper cup of tea and get the taste of stir chuck washed out of you.

Idly he strolled along with the cockney strut becoming more pronounced at every step. What the hell? He was a London bloke all right and nobody could say he wasn't. Even if he had done one or two little things he was as wide a boy as they made them.

Just to prove it he walked across the road in and out of the traffic half a dozen or so times, and then, after being cursed at by taxi drivers, bus drivers, van drivers and cyclists, he gave it up. Anybody who watched him might think that he'd done his nut or something the way he was going on. Besides, if a bogey lamped him he'd do him in two two's. If you crossed the road too often they was bound to say you were loitering with intent to commit a felony.

He took his cigarette from behind his ear, lit it and strolled into a coffee bar.

'Tea, please,' he said, banging two coppers down on the counter.

'Well, I don't know.' The counterman paused in his

conversation with the only other customer and, taking a cup that already contained milk and sugar, held it beneath an urn, filled it with steaming tea and, having handed it to Shorty, was ready to go on talking. 'You got to have a law. I mean to say where'd we all be if you hadn't of got a law. Take you and me now. We can sleep peacefully at home at nights. Why?'

'Because you ain't got a lodger,' said Shorty, stirring his tea and wishing they wouldn't gup so much.

'I'll tell you why,' the counterman was used to being interrupted, 'because we got law and order. Not that I ain't sorry for him, mind you, but still you got to have an example. If you didn't have an example, where'd you be?'

'Yerce.' His listener was not quite convinced. 'That's all right. You got to have an example, granted. But what I say's this. What'd they want to go and hang that poor bloke Allen for? He'd been all right. Only made one mistake in his life and he has to go and get hung. That's what I say. What they want to do is to go and knock off some of these blokes that go around killing girls in Soho. Why, gor blimey all bloody hurray, easiest thing you can do nowadays is to pick up with some tart and do her in. Not that they're any bloody good to themselves or anyone else admitted, but they're entitled to protection same as you and me.'

Shorty sipped his tea. It was so hot that he couldn't drink it fast enough to suit him. He'd like to get out of this gaff as quick as he could. It put years on him to listen to these two mugs yammering away like a pair of monkeys.

Another bloke came in. He was wearing a green hat perched on the side of his head and a wisp of hair hung down over his left temple. He had a blue-and-white spotted silk handkerchief round his neck. He rubbed his hands together and blew on them to make them warmer.

'Cup o' tea, mate,' he said, 'and make it hot. 'Tain't half

bleeding cold outside, and make it a bit sharpish and all. I left me barrer outside. Copped out twice last week for obstruction. Bleeding mustard they're getting now. Don't give a bloke a chance to earn an honest living. Trying to make you turn bloody crooked, that's what they're doing.'

'Tell you what it is,' said the counterman, self-opinionated as ever, 'it's all this here rearmament. They puts the blokes inside on making sailors' hammocks, ships' fenders, haversacks for soldiers and all that caper, and the more they knock off the happier they are.'

The coster took his cup of tea and, turning away from the counter, got a full view of Shorty's face. He grinned with happy recognition.

'Blimey, mate. Didn't see you. How you getting on? All right? That's the way.' He shook him vigorously by the hand and went on talking without giving Shorty any chance to answer. ''Member that tart you used to go with. You know the one with a turned-up nose. Alice. I seen her once or twice lately. Yerce. Lives around here and all now. Don't half get up to some capers with the boys. You want to put a stop to that a bit sharpish, mate. She'll be getting herself into trouble one of these next days. Drummond Street, she lives. Just round the corner. Well, round the back. Well, so long. I'll get meself done if you keep me talking to you any more. Ta ta. Look after yourself.'

He darted off into the street and caught hold of the handles of his barrow. Shorty yelled after him to find out the number in Drummond Street. Pushing his barrow along, the coster yelled it back and then burst into his customary call, regardless of the fact that it was a cold February day and he was selling apples.

'Strawberry. Strawberry. Strawberry. We shan't be round tomorrow, the donkey's dead. Strawberry. Straw . . . berry. Ripe strawberry.'

'D'you know Len?' asked the counterman. 'Star turn,

23

ain't he? Don't give no other bastards a chance to say a blind word.'

'Yerce. I know him all right. Morning.'

Shorty walked out into the main drag again. He was feeling better for the warm tea in his stomach. Soon it would be opening time and he could go and have a pint and a nice game of darts. Have a chat with one or two of the boys and then maybe take a girl to the pictures. That was a nice little day. What the hell had he got to be so browned off about? He ought to be feeling proper chirpy.

Alice. Hell of a time since he'd seen Alice. Twenty-one moon. Five hundred and forty-three days in stir. Three weeks on remand first. That made it eighty weeks and it must have been five weeks before he'd got knocked off that he'd had that quarrel with Alice. Put it down as five hundred and ninety-nine days. For a sentence of two years you only did six hundred and twelve days. Nice little bit Alice had been and all. Drummond Street. Gorblimey O'Reilly that was a come down for her.

He looked distastefully at the shabby street in which he found himself. Funny thing, somehow or another he'd already strayed into Drummond Street. Hadn't meant to. Must of done it just by thinking about Alice. It just showed you what figuring out all those bloody numbers did to you. Well, since he was here, he might as well go and look her up. What was the number Len had said?

He rang the bell at a dirty door beside a sad-looking shop.

Right looking gaff to be living in.

There was no answer. He rang the bell again. No answer again. He rang a third time, listening to hear if the bell rang. It didn't seem to. He rapped on the panels of the door with his knuckles. Slowly the door swung open. Whoever had gone in or come out last time hadn't closed it properly. Right sort of a screwsman he was, not to notice a thing like that. Well, if the door was open he might as well walk in.

He walked across the narrow hallway. At the end was a door. Well, that would be where the old woman who kept the shop lived. No sense in going there, except perhaps on the way down just to see if there was anything worth knocking off.

He climbed the dingy stairs and came to the first landing. There were two doors. He opened them both. Both rooms were empty. Probably they belonged to other lodgers for the beds were were tousled and unmade. It wasn't like Alice to be going out so early in the morning. He climbed up to the second landing. It was filthy, dark and smelt of stale frying. There was a dirty old gas cooker in what little space there was and a couple of penny-in-the-slot meters. Shorty ran a professional eye over them. Hardly worth the risk of doing it. Not penny meters. All he'd do would be to cop a dollar's worth of coppers.

He opened the back-room door.

The blue blind hung half-way down over the window. It was too dark to see anything properly. It looked as if somebody were in bed. He went over and let up the blind. It ran up unevenly and stuck again, but enough grey light came through the exposed panes to show the cold room in all its cheap ugliness.

Alice was lying on the bed. She was lying very still and all. She must have been on a proper night out. Blimey, she'd got a silk stocking wound round her neck. Fear touched him with its icy fingers. He tiptoed over to the bed.

Outed she was all right. Somebody must of done her in.

For a moment he stood there, calmly acquiescent, and then he began to panic. If they found him here they'd charge him with it for certain. How long had she been dead?

Allen was dead. She was dead. Somebody had strangled her and the hangman had strangled Allen. The hangman would have a go at him, too. He ran his tongue over his lips.

Gawd almighty. Gawd. Let me out of this. Let me get out of here.

He bit his parched lips to prevent himself from yelling.

How long had she been dead? Nobody could pin it on him if she'd been dead a long time. He had a water-tight alibi. There's no better one in all the world than being in stir. All he had to do was use his nut.

Wrapping his handkerchief round his hand to prevent fingerprints, he started to work. Well, it wasn't going to be nice, but he'd got to do it. He picked up her bag which was lying on the floor. The mirror was cracked, the powder spilt. There were one or two letters, and the front-door key. No money.

Well, he'd got to do it. The point was when had she kicked off? He knelt down beside the bed. Blimey, this was a terrible job and no mistake. Softly and with almost reverential tenderness he laid his cheek against hers.

Christ! It was still faintly warm.

He got up again. His knees were dusty.

Well, that was that. That was that. She couldn't of bin done in long. Probably kicked off just after Allen. Certainly late enough for them to pin it on him. He had to get out of it. That's what he had to do. Go and show himself in places. No, keep out of places. No, act normal.

He looked round the room. Somehow or other he was scared to leave the place. There must be something here to prove it wasn't him.

On the table stood half a loaf, an opened tin of salmon, two dirty plates, two used glasses and a practically empty bottle of cheap red Australian wine. Well, the story was clear enough. Any mug could see it. She'd got a bit lit up the night before and lumbered someone back. He'd spent the night, done her in, grabbed her dough and scrammed. It couldn't have been very long since he'd made his get-away. That had been the reason for the front door being not properly closed. The geezer had been in such a hurry that he'd left it open.

Well, that didn't help him any. All he had to do was get out of it. They'd never think of him unless they actually caught him in the gaff. It was easy. All he had to do was act as if it were an ordinary day and he had just come out of the nick. Poor Alice. He looked at her. Well, whatever had happened to her she wouldn't be getting into any more jams. That was one thing that was certain sure.

He pushed his hat on to the back of his head and looked at her again.

Come on, son, snap out of it. You'll get yourself done if you stick around any longer. Get going.

Still he reluctantly lingered. While he was between four walls he felt safe. Outside in the open, anybody might be getting at him.

Don't talk berkish. Get out of it while you can.

He tiptoed across the room, and pausing at the door, he took one more look at Alice. Poor kid. She'd had a tough break. Always liked a joke too.

He took off his hat and then stuck it savagely on his head again. Blimey, he was acting proper soft. He walked downstairs trying to act as if nothing had happened.

On the landing below a door opened and a woman was waiting for him with her arms on her hips. She had thin, greyish hair and a wart on her cheek. Her lips curled sarcastically.

'Well, young man?' she said in her old-maidish voice. 'And what are you doing here, if I may ask?'

'Good morning,' Shorty muttered and tried to get past her.

'Not so fast, young man, not so fast. First you explain

to me what you're doing in my house. Up to no good, I'll be bound.'

'Bin upstairs. Bin seeing a young lady.'

Blimey, there he'd gone and made a bloomer. Well, what the hell else could he say anyway? Probably the old dear was used to her lodgers having men visitors.

'Oh, you have, have you? And it's that Alice, I'll lay. The little madam. The impertinence of it. As soon as she took the room I said to her, "None of your tricks, Miss," I said, "I know your sort," I said, "and I hope I'm broad-minded. It takes all sorts to make a world and I know it as well as you do, but I'm not going to have any of your goings-on under my roof," I said. "Do what you like, but do it else-where," I said. I've had my suspicions of that piece for some time and I'm not going to stand for it no more. It's not as though she's paid me a penny-piece more rent for the men she's brought back either. Now, mind you, I'm a respectable woman myself, but if she'd have come to me straight and said "I had two gentleman friends back today so here's an extra half a crown on top of the rent," well I wouldn't have done nothing. It's this underhandedness. Not playing the game, that's what I call it.'

'All right, ma. All right,' said Shorty trying to put over a line of bluff geniality. 'Now let's get out of here.'

But the landlady had not yet finished her say.

'Well as I been saying I've had my ideas this long time past but I've kept them to myself. "Least said, soonest mended," that's what I said to myself, but now I'm going to walk upstairs and tell that flibbertigibbet exactly what I think of her.'

Her foot was already on the lowest stair when Shorty was past her and before she had opened Alice's door he was in the street.

CHAPTER III

Shorty sat in the News Theatre. It was comfortably dark in there. He'd already seen the pictures round three times, but until he could think of a more reassuring place to lounge around in he was staying. All he hoped was that one of the usherettes didn't fluff to him and call the chucker-out.

There was a dame sitting next to him. She had one nicely-rounded leg crossed over the other! From her there came a nice smell of face powder and perfume. When he had looked at her first, she had turned away and he had seen just how prettily her nose tilted upwards. Then, during the Silly Symphony she had laughed and turned towards him, but somehow he hadn't the heart to do anything about it. She must think him a proper softy. He lit a cigarette and tried to think things out.

The sensible thing to do was to go outside and buy an evening paper and see what they had to say about it. The old dear was bound to have given his description. He was better off sitting inside in the warmth, than outside hearing the bloody worst. This was the hell of a thing to happen to a man on the day he'd just come out and was entitled to take things easy and have a bit of fun.

The two detectives lit their pipes from the same match.

'Well,' said the elder, 'that ought to do it. Description in all the papers and broadcast in the news tonight. We'll get him all right. Get him before morning I shouldn't wonder. Damned good job too. I'm getting just about sick of all these cracks about anybody being able to go and knock off one of the girls. This'll do us a bit of good.'

'Yes,' the younger's voice was a little dubious. 'Think he really did it, though? Somehow it doesn't ring true to me.'

'True enough, man. It's an open and shut case. There's his fingerprint on the windowpane . . .'

'Yerce, but there's different dabs on the tumblers.'

'They may be old ones. There's the landlady's identification. And there's the fact he's known to have mucked in with the girl before he went to prison. He went there to tap her and she wouldn't come across, so he did her in and helped himself.'

'S'pose so.'

'S'pose so? Why it's clear as crystal. He's done it all right. There's the statement from that costermonger, Len. I thought he'd had a hand in it myself, but he tells us that he gave the address to Mr Shorty Mathews this morning. Right customer, young Shorty. Hasn't been out of prison two hours before he's committed a murder. But we'll get him, easy as easy.'

The early afternoon editions of the papers had the following headlines on their posters:

STRANGLED GIRL

MAN'S DESCRIPTION

A thin man in a shabby raincoat bought a copy at Clapham Junction. He opened the pages with trembling fingers, but as he read elation and relief crept into his heart. His lips slavered as he walked along.

Shorty bought a copy in Charing Cross Road. His heart sank. The railway stations and the motor coaches would be covered. It was the road for him. He fingered the coins in his pocket. He had seven shillings and fivepence.

CHAPTER IV

The street lights made the rain-damped road a glistening and shiny black as it ran uphill and down, but ever northward through the little town that had risen from the status of a market town to a suburb. Shorty trudged along with his coat collar turned up and his hands deep in his trousers pockets. Inconsequently his thoughts ran on.

When you got knocked off you never knew what sort of a sentence you were going to draw. Twenty-one moon made the seasons go all wrong. You went in in summer clothes and came out in the winter. If they topped you it was different, you come out wearing nothing, you didn't have to worry any more, that was one thing. All these blokes now had homes to go to, and overcoats to wear, and they went to work regular, and stood about on the pavements of their own town as if it belonged to them, which it did all said and done, so you couldn't expect them to move out of your way. Look at Woolworth's now, making a great patch of light. And the blokes selling evening papers. And the women with shopping bags. It was a bastard all ways up when you come to think about it. Blokes worked and what did they get? Nothing but bloody misery, and the old woman going out shopping and carrying home the parcels and trying to get twenty-five og out of a green one, and all the same it was better than being on the crook and wondering all the time what was going to happen next.

He shook his head so that a dewdrop would fall off the end of his nose. It was far too cold for him to take his hands out of his pockets. As he walked he limped a little because his left shoe was beginning to give water. It had been a hell of a long walk so far even if he had taken a pennorth on a tram three times. The road forked and he stood undecided, looking at the signpost. One arm pointed to The North and the other to St Albans.

Well, there was one for you. Which was the best road to take? Oh hell, any road was all right just so long as it didn't go back to the Smoke. No, use your crust, kid. It was getting late and all and it was a hell of a cold night to do a skipper. Just outside this town on one of these roads there was a café where all the transport drivers pulled in. That was the joint to make for. Well, it was stone ginger that it was on the road north. Yes, but the only time he'd bin to that caff the wagon had come through St Albans. Weigh that one up. Yerce, sort it out. And hurry up about it and all. It was a dead certain way of getting knocked off standing at street corners looking spare. And if there was just one thing that Mr Shorty Mathews just couldn't afford, why blimey it was to be lifted.

While he had been standing by the signpost three lorries had lumbered past him bearing left along the St Albans road. Well, blimey, that settled it. It was St Albans then.

He set off. Almost immediately the road became darker. There were no shops now along the way, only private houses and an occasional street lamp. Somehow or another this made it even colder than before. Lorries passed him more and more frequently. A man came out of his house and looked at him curiously before he got into his parked car. If it had not been so nippy Shorty would have begun to feel sleepy. Back in stir most of the boys would be putting their bed boards down and getting into kip. He had not had much snore the night before. Lorries passed him with a whizz and a roar. An occasional man on a bike toiled past with bowed head.

A road sign with a diagonal stripe on it, showing the

end of a restricted area, loomed up in front of him. On his side of the road the pavement had ended. He was in the country now. Blimey, when was that caff going to show up? For some reason there was a pavement on the other side. He crossed over.

The houses had all ended and there were now fields bordering the road. It was very much colder and Shorty was shivering as he walked. He was glad that there was a pavement beneath his feet. A London bloke who was used to pavements and street lights and houses all round him felt a bit out of it in the country. He shied like a frightened horse at a tree that was growing in the hedge.

Way ahead of him on the left he could see the lights of a house. Must be about a mile off. He made a bet with himself. As soon as he reached that house something good would happen to him. He was limping badly now. The long thin-toed yellowish-brown shoes that he was wearing had been built for standing outside coffee stalls, not for trudging along country roads. The rain was coming down quite heavily, being blown across the fields in angry gusts. Something good had just got to happen to him. That was all there was to it.

As he topped a slight rise he saw that the house was a pub and outside the pub a lorry was drawn up. Well, if the driver wouldn't give him a lift anyway he would be able to have half a pint and sit by the fire for a bit. A cyclist passed him, battling his way with difficulty through the rain-lashed crosswind.

Soaked through and limping, Shorty reached the pub. On the opposite side of the road was a filling station. He could see a couple of lads larking about in the warm garage and a pang of envy for the comfortable and unworried filled his heart as he stood with his hand on the brass door-knob of the public bar.

He sighed, opened the door and went in. A lad was

sitting on a bench by the fire, eating bread and cheese. An old labourer was sitting in the corner with a pint on the table in front of him. He was cutting up plug tobacco with the blackened blade of his knife. Both of them glanced incuriously at Shorty as he went over to the hatch and called for his half pint of ale.

'Wet old night, mate,' said the labourer as Shorty sat down.

'Yerce.'

'Proper bastard,' said the youth.

Shorty turned to him.

'That your lorry outside, mate?'

'Yerce, the green one.'

'Going far?'

'Leicester.'

'Any chance of giving us a ride?'

'Sorry, mate, I can't. Me guv'nor's over on the other side. There's only room for two. Besides he's bloody mustard against giving lifts. Where you want to get to?'

'Up north,' Shorty was purposely vague.

'Yerce? Well, you ought to get some transport all right. There's bags of stuff on the road.'

'Ain't there a caff on the road somewhere about here where they all pull in?'

'That's right,' said the labourer, slowly. He was teasing up his tobacco now between the palms of his horny hands. 'Two mile up the road.'

'Two mile? Blimey, it's a rough old drop of weather to walk a couple of bleeding miles.'

'Weather ain't what it used to be years ago,' said the labourer. 'Why I can remember when you dursent go out for a week.'

'If it's two miles it's two short bastards,' said the young lorry driver. 'Besides there's a bus goes there, ain't there?'

'Passes the door,' said the old man, slowly tamping down the tobacco into his clay pipe.

'Bound to get a lift there, aren't I?' said Shorty.

'Certain to, mate. Stick around there long enough and you're bound to find somebody who'll see you all right.'

The labourer took the match away from his pipe. It was glowing nicely now.

'There's your bus now,' he said. 'Stopped outside.'

Shorty gulped down his beer and rushed out. He hopped the bus just as it was starting. That was something that a city-bred bloke could do even when he was in the country.

'You go near a transport caff, don't you, mate?' he said to the conductor before he mounted the stairs to the upper deck.

'Penny,' said the conductor, briefly clanging his punch and handing out the ticket.

On the top deck were sitting three lads. They were singing 'Little Old Lady', and trying to harmonize. Well, they must have got something to be happy about. Suddenly, ahead, there was a blaze of lights. It must be here that the café was, just where another road crossed the Great North Road. Well, that old labourer sure had a funny idea about just how long two miles might be.

Shorty climbed down off the bus and stood on the pavement, trying to see exactly what he had to do. Ahead of him, the other side of the traffic lights, was a garage and filling station. Outside it, in great neon lights, blazed the words SPROCKETT'S CORNER. An enterprising tradesman was trying to perpetuate his name. One day it was going to be part of the geography of England. On the right was an open space of ground on which a number of laden lorries were drawn up. Beyond the parking space, brilliantly lighted, as everything else in this district seemed to be, was a two-storied building. It was the café.

Plodding through the churned-up black mud, Shorty made his way to the café. He glanced at one or two of the lorries. Glossop's, Sheffield, he read. London Scottish Road Transport Company, Elgins, Manchester, Lancashire Contract and Traction. Well, if he couldn't get a lift here, he was a bit slow and that was all there was to it.

Above the catch of the glass door leading to the café hung a mud-bespattered, rain-soaked piece of cardboard – 'Lift and Push'. Shorty lifted, pushed and went inside.

'Close the door, can't you?'

He closed the door and looked around the room. A familiar sour smell filled his nose. What was it? Where had he come across it before? Sweaty bodies, an open coke fire, cheap clothes drying from the rain, coarse dirty fat used for frying eggs. Why, the joint smelt exactly like a cheap kip-house. A large part of the floor was sanded, and in one corner stood an old grand piano. There was a flight of stairs leading up to the second storey. The counter was semi-circular and a couple of men in dirty white coats were standing behind it. There was a ring of chairs by the fire. A couple of drivers were playing draughts and another three were grouped round their table, watching them. Another half a dozen stood around the pin-tables, gambling.

Shorty went up to the counter, paid three ha'pence for a cup of tea and went over to the fire to get warm. There was no need to hurry over getting himself some transport. Over the fireplace hung two notices. One in red said:

BEDS IS. 6D.

The other in blue pencil read:

CUSTOMERS ARE NOT ALLOWED TO SLEEP IN
THE CAFE. BEDS ARE PROVIDED AT VERY
NOMINAL CHARGES

He sat down in a vacant chair, next to a young driver who was picking his teeth with a sharpened matchstick and reading a tattered copy of a morning newspaper which bore the impress of an iron-studded heel.

'Going north, mate?' asked Shorty.

'No. Kipping here tonight.'

Another bloke glanced at him. He was sitting with his chair tilted back on to its two rear legs.

'Watchew want, china? A ride?'

'Yerce. Can you give us one?'

'Where going?'

'Up north.'

'No, mate. I'm kipping here tonight and all. You don't stand much chance here of copping a ride tonight. Most of the blokes is on their way to the Smoke or else taking a kip. Too near London this is for a bloke to stop off at on his way up. Not unless he's done his eleven hours and wants to take a kip. Might touch lucky though. You never know.'

Shorty pulled a dog end out of his pocket and lit it. He was beginning to feel depressed. It didn't seem that he was meant to have any luck. He drank his tea slowly, trying to think out the best thing to do. Maybe if he went around the pin-tables he might touch lucky. There was quite a number of blokes there now. He went over, with his tea cup in his hand, and watched the players. One geezer had just copped a packet of five Players by winning on the action.

'Duff old machines these,' said a driver who had pushed his peaked cap on to the back of his head. 'Whyn't they gets some new'uns? Blimey, there's all those electric bastards with bumpers and all. That's what they want to get.'

'That's right, mate,' said Shorty, who had not the ghost of a notion what was being talked about. They must have brought out a lot of new machines since he had gone inside. 'You going north?'

'Where you want to get to?'

'Sheffield,' said Shorty at random.

'No, mate, I'm going to Manchester.'

'Manchester? That'd do me fine.'

'Hell of a long way off of Sheffield. I'm going on the Coventry road. You want to get on to one of the Glossop blokes. They go up to Sheffield direct, or else one of the Jocks. They go up Doncaster way.'

'Thanks, mate,' said Shorty discouragedly.

For a little while he sipped his chilling tea and watched the drivers gambling. Penny after penny was fed into the machines, but no lucky numbers turned.

'Proper money-making lark this,' said Shorty.

'That's reet, chum,' said a middle-aged man with a flat northern accent. 'The bloke that owns these has five men employed working for him. Retired lieutenant-commander from the navy.'

'Going north?'

'Nay, chum. I'm off for London in a few minutes. Tha'll be reet lucky to get a ride north tonight.'

'Any Aberdonian blokes here?' shouted out one of the countermen.

'Aye! What's wrang?' A short thick-set Scot answered.

'You're wanted on the blower.'

The Scotty went behind the counter, answered the telephone and came back to touch one of his mates on the shoulder.

'Alf,' he said, 'they want you.'

'Going north, mate?' asked Shorty desperately.

'No. I'm kipping here the night and going into the Smoke the morn. Ma mate's going north to Glasgow though if you want a ride. The bloke that's on the blower the noo.'

'Thanks, mate, you're a toff.'

'He'll gie you a ride as like as not, but there's no need to say I said so, though.'

'Okay, mate.'

When Alf came from behind the counter, Shorty button-holed him.

'Going north, mate?'

'Yerce. Soon's I've done a bit of reloading. Watchew want? A lift?'

'That's right.'

'Well, you have a cold bloody ride then. There's no glass in the cab. Where you want to get to?'

'Sheffield.'

Shorty had been thinking quickly. There was no sense in saying he wanted to go to Glasgow. This bloke was bound to know the town and it might be a bit awkward.

'Well, I'll give you a ride's far's Doncaster if you like.'

He went over and spoke to his mates. Shorty stood around nervously.

'Okay, mate,' said Alf. 'Come and give us a hand with this reloading. My firm's just been on the blower. I got to take on a load off of Charley here.' He raised his voice. 'Here, Charley, come here a minute.'

Charley and Jock left the pin-table and Shorty took the opportunity of going to the urinal. Among the usual drawings and *facetiae* scrawled on the walls were the words: 'A Miss in the cab is worth two in the engine.' Smiling, he went back into the café. The three Aberdonian drivers were just leaving the place so Shorty followed them out of the door into the parking space. Out there the north-east wind cut like a knife. He shivered and glanced upwards at the cloudy sky.

'Blimey, Jock,' he said, trying to make conversation, 'shouldn't wonder if it come on to snow.'

The Scotty grunted and swung himself up into the cab of a lorry.

'I'll bring her alongside yourn, Alf,' he said, 'just gie us a swing.'

Alf cranked the starting handle and Jock backed his wagon through the churned-up freezing mud until it stood head to tail with another lorry.

'Come on, chum,' said Charley, 'give us a hand getting these here bleeding sheets off. Unfasten the ropes.'

With numb fingers Shorty worked awkwardly at the knots of the ropes. Jock and Alf had undone and coiled the ropes and lifted back the tarpaulin sheets off one wagon before Charley and Shorty had finished untying the knots.

'Come on, mate,' said Charley. 'Blimey, you're just like an old woman, straight you are. Put a bit of jildy into it for Christ's sake. I don't want to be here in the bleeding cold all night.'

At last both lorries were unsheeted. One was laden with bathtubs and the other with oblong sacks.

'Here,' said Jock, swinging himself up on to the bathtub lorry, 'gie us a hand, chum. We'll stack.'

Charley and Alf climbed on to the other lorry and working together began to sling the sacks over. Shorty, helping Jock stack them among the bathtubs, soon forgot to wish he was wearing an overcoat. The sacks, heavy and filled with something unresisting, were quite enough to keep his mind busy as he worked. His hands were soft from twenty-one months in prison and his muscles were quite unused to heavy work. Charley and Alf were working rhythmically, not straining themselves, but slinging over the sacks at a fair pace. When Shorty's heart was beating so fast that he thought it was going to burst he took a rest, supporting himself with one hand on the top of the cab.

'What's in these bastards for Christ's sake?' he asked, kicking a sack.

'Rubber. Raw rubber.'

'Blimey, I thought it was sides of bacon.'

'They wouldna be so light if they were sides of bacon. You'd have a job handling them. Come on, for Christ's sake. Get stuck into it. You must have been galloping your antelope, I'm thinking.'

Shorty got stuck into it. Charley and Alf jumped over and gave them a hand. Charley had a moan as usual. All the time he worked he chatted.

'Never bin on such a firm in all me life. Trust Scotch blokes to be messing you about. You a Jock, mate?'

'No, I'm a London bloke.'

'What part d'you come from?'

'Walworth.'

'I come from Acton meself. If you're a London bloke what the hell do you want to go north for? Blimey, I should have thought you'd of known better than that. Don't know when you're well off some of you people. That's the trouble. Come on, give us a hand to sling this bastard up on top there. Easy now. You don't want to rupture your bleeding self, do you? Never seen such a firm, not in all my days. Come down from Aberdeen this morning with a load and they say "Sorry Charley you'll have to take another packet north" and loads up me wagon with this here bleeding rubber. "Do what, mate?" I says. "I'm entitled to one kip same as all the other drivers. Where'd me log sheets be? I'll take this here load out and kip at a caff." So me and Alf starts off. We stops here and the firm gets on the blower. I've only got to reload my rubber on Alf's wagon and he takes the lot up and tomorrow I got to go back to the Smoke and pick up a fresh packet. Messing a bloke about all the time, that's what they're doing. Well, mate, that's about the lot. We only got to get the sheets on now. I don't envy you, I must say, taking a ride on this bitch. Cold bloody cab it is with the windows out.'

They hopped down off the wagon and fixed the sheets.

Alf swung himself into the cab. The engine had been ticking over during the hour that they had worked.

'Come on, china,' he shouted above the rattle and the roar. 'Hop on board now. We're off.'

Shorty hopped in beside Alf. The lorry swung its snub nose out of the parking space and started off, past the lights of Sprockett's Corner, on its long, cold journey north.

CHAPTER V

A big green lorry was pulling out of Coventry for Grimsby. The driver sat erect over his wheel and cursed as a private car dashed past him without dimming its lights. On the other side of the engine sat a girl, whose imitation fur collar was turned up around her ears. Her feet, in patent-leather slippers with trodden-down heels, and her legs in well-darned Woolworth's stockings were frozen. Her blue eyes were bleary and puffy from want of sleep. She crouched towards the engine to keep herself warm. Fred, the driver, misinterpreted her motive.

'That's a good gel,' he said, yelling to make himself heard. 'We'll get together just as soon as we're on the road a piece. You know the old driver's motto, don't you? A Miss in the cab is worth two in the engine.'

He chuckled and then looked ahead, concentrating on his driving. He had to be at Grimsby by two in the morning if he wanted to get his load of fish back to Worcester in time. Coventry. Caw. It was a stroke of luck that he had thought of making the journey round the long way. Bound to bloody well touch lucky you was at Coventry. Take plenty of explaining away it would though. Artful bastard the guv'nor. Got one of them secret clocks put in so he knew just how many miles a bloke went and when he stopped and for how long. Ah well. You had to box clever. A log sheet could be fiddled. Another bloody private roaring past without dimming. Got no consideration some bastards hadn't.

The girl opened her handbag with her red, chapped fingers. Mean bastard this driver. Didn't even give a girl a smoke. Just because he stood a cup of tea in the caff he thought he was okay. Bleeding well learn where he was mistaken.

She fumbled in the darkness among the old letters, the lipstick, the three ha'pence and the box of cheap powder that she had in her bag for the crumpled green packet of cigarettes. There ought to be one fag left. She found it and stuck it between her wind-cracked lips. No matches, though.

'Here, mate,' she leant over the engine and touched Big Fred on the arm. 'Got a match?'

He grinned and drove on.

'Yes, thanks.'

'Well, give us a light then.'

'Give us a fag and all, kid.'

'Ain't got none. This here's me last.'

'Gaw blimey, you can't half tell the tale. Straight up.'

'Well, I ain't got none. May I never get up off of this seat. So there.'

'All right, all right. I believe you. Thousands wouldn't.' He stuck his gloved hand down into his overcoat pocket. ''Ere y'are. Box of lights coming up.'

He handed the girl a box of matches. She lit her cigarette and, silently restoring the box to its owner, smoked on. Every time she drew in her smoke, her pale flour-coated cheeks hollowed. The noise of the engine was getting monotonous.

The only thing that kept her awake was the headlights that kept glaring through the windscreen. One thing about this wagon though. It hadn't got such a draughty cab as the bastard she had driven down from Carlisle on. The driver had taken the western route instead of going across through Richmond and Boroughbridge and down by Doncaster. He had dropped her off at Coventry. Half a dollar he had given her and cheap at the price too. All day long she had sat about in Coventry, in a café. None of the drivers had dared to give her a ride while it was still daylight. The police were getting mustard about lorry gels now. She'd get this bloke to drop her off in Nottingham, at Trent Bridge. There was no sense in going on to the Great North Road. The coppers were hotter along that toby than anywhere else in England.

She had spent the half-crown on food and cups of tea. None of the boys had even staked her to a cup of tea. Right mingy lot of bastards. She would ask this geezer for half a quid. If he come across she'd be able to buy a new pair of cami-knicks. That bloke in Preston had been ever so rough. What time was he going to get to Nottingham? It was a bastard town to be stranded in after eleven. Before that you stood a good chance of picking up a mug who'd pay the hotel bill and give you half a quid or even fifteen bob. Once she had got off with a bloke there and he and his pal had taken her for a ride in a private car and each of them had dropped her a oncer.

'What time do you reckon on getting to Nottingham, dear?' she yelled.

'You're dead out of luck, Kiddo,' he hollered back. 'I don't go through Nottingham. Drop you off at Newark if you like.'

'Yeah? Don't talk wet. Drop me off at Coventry on your way back.'

'Ain't going to Coventry, my old darling.'

She shrugged her shoulders and puffed on her cigarette. First she tried sitting with her hands folded between her knees and then she crossed her arms. She could not get warm anyway. There was still a stink of fish coming from the back part of the wagon although it was running empty except for a load of baskets and crates.

Mile after mile was ticked off by the speedometer and the secret clock. They rode in silence for neither had much to say and it was tough work talking loud enough to be heard. Twice Fred lit a cigarette, once he gave the girl one. She accepted it nonchalantly and without a word of thanks.

What the hell, she was thinking. Grimsby, that's a town to stop off at. Ask for a bit of plaice with two eyes in it just to see me over the weekend. First caff he stopped at she'd duck. Blimey, surely the miserable bastard intended buying a cup of tea. She would hop off there and leave him. With any luck she could get another ride to Coventry. It would be nice to take a spin down to the Smoke and then a trip along the West to Bristol or Cardiff. Cardiff was all right. She had a nice time there and then she went to live with that nigger bloke from the West Indies. Lovely time they had and he'd treated her good and all before he had to go and get himself knocked off for drawing the dole and him not even entitled to be signing on at the Labour. This bloke was making good time. Well, he ought to be and all with no load to speak of and a brand new Bedford. If only she could get hold of a little money now she'd spend it right. Get her hair permed, just the ends, that was enough. You could get off all right if your hair looked nice under your hat. Riding in wagons you didn't have to take your hat off. Even if you was on the game in a town there was no need to take it off until you'd got the steamer to pay up. A pair of shoes and all and them new cami-knickers. Blimey, she'd like to show that cat Elsie up. Dancing around the café like a big cow, showing all the boys her cami-knicks and yelling out and carrying on at all the other girls to do the same just because she knew she was the only girl in the place that had got a clean pair on. Proper little Madam that Elsie. Like to scratch the cat's eyes out and that time in Dunstable too . . .

Ahead of them were the lights of a café. Fred brought his lorry to a standstill on the pull-in. He leant over the engine to talk to Molly.

'Just going in to get a cup of tea,' he said, still shouting as though the engine were running. 'Don't you come in and all or they might think there was something funny on. They ain't half getting hot about the girls just now. I'll bring you out a cup.'

She stiffened petulantly.

'I want to go and sit by the fire,' she whined.

'Well, you can't then, so there,' he said brusquely. 'You heard.'

'Proper Mr Cautious, ain't you?' she sneered.

Fred, who by this time had his cab door open and one foot on the wheel, paused. The blow at his pride had made him wince.

'Tell you what I'll do. I'll bring you out a bacon sandwich and all, so there. That ought to satisfy.'

She relented. After all he was right. She didn't know this road and they might be right bastards on the girls.

'Bring us out a large Player and all, dear,' she said, putting her head on one side and smiling. 'I ain't got no fags left.'

Might as well try to soak the bastard for all I can get. Wonder if he'll be good for half a quid. Half a dollar looks more like his mark. Half dollars aren't much bleeding use. Costs very near that for a day's expenses and I'll have to be getting a new pair of stockings. Where would this dump be? Miles out somewhere. Bloke ain't half being a time over that cup of tea and bacon sandwich. Sitting by the fire and getting a good warm. Didn't even leave me a fag. Now if a girl could get two rides a day and each one stand her a feed and drop a dollar she'd be on velvet. Not that there was much to this being a road girl. You was better off in a town all said and done. All this riding up and down the country wasn't much good. The best thing was to hang on to any dough you got and get a room in a town somewhere. Bristol or Brum or Norwich or Nottingham.

Anywhere where they didn't mess you about too much. It was all right going on the road when you was a kid. Nice to travel around the country a bit and the drivers seemed like aeroplane pilots, but what did you get out of it all said and done? Only cold and crabs. It wasn't any bottle when you got a bit older. If you didn't watch out you turned into an old mare like Coventry Cis.

Fred came out of the café walking carefully. In one hand he was carrying a cup of tea, in the other a bacon sandwich carefully wrapped in a piece of grease-proof paper so that it was not soiled by contact with his grease-stained fingers.

He opened the cab door on her side, and climbed up on the wheel. 'Here y'are, kid,' he said. 'Don't say I ain't generous.'

She took the cup from him and the sandwich. Some tea slopped into the saucer.

'Get the fags?'

'Sure.'

He tossed a packet of twenty cigarettes on to her lap. She smiled at him and he smiled back vacuously. He looked the sort of bloke a girl could string along. She poured the tea from the saucer into the cup and began to drink with noisy sips. Greedily Fred stood there watching. She wasn't a bad-looking piece. He would park on that grass verge about a mile up the road and give her a tumble. She stripped the paper off the sandwich and bit into the fat, salty bacon in the grease-soaked bread. Standing there with only a row of petrol pumps to keep him from the wind, Fred felt cold.

'Come on, kid,' he said, 'there's a good girl. Drink up that tea and we'll get started. 'Tain't half bleeding cold.'

'Took your time yourself, dincha? Men!'

Nevertheless she gulped down her tea and handed Fred back the cup. By the time he had carried it into the shanty and come back into the cab she had finished the sandwich too, and had a cigarette between her lips.

'Give us a light, ducks, before you start. There's a love.'

Fred lit her cigarette for her and laid his hand on hers clumsily. His pulses were throbbing. Proper little piece she was and all. Bet she'd had a few men in her time.

'What's your name, kid?' he asked huskily. Excitement had made his voice so dry that he found it quite a job to speak.

'Molly.'

Saucily she puffed smoke into his face. He grabbed at her wrist, but she dodged him with a toss of her wispy blonde hair.

'Naughty girl, ain'tcher?' Fred grinned delightedly.

'Didn't you ought to be getting started?' she said.

'Ah well. S'pose I might as well.'

Fred climbed down from the cab again, cranked the engine, climbed back and started off. His driving was more erratic now, for his hands were unsteady and his brain racing. Well, she was going to see what kind of a man he was and damned quick too. Molly sat, drawing on her cigarette, and wishing that he had not made her hurry so over her tea. A bacon sandwich and nothing to drink after it left you thirsty.

Suddenly Fred drew his lorry up on a grass verge and put out his headlights. It was not likely that there would be any speed cops about.

'Watchew stopping for?'

'You know.'

Fred was climbing over the engine to Molly's side of the cab. His heart was beating so hard that he was certain that she would hear it and think he was a softy. Molly herself sat still in the darkness with a resigned look on her face.

Ah well s'pose it was going to be the same thing all

over again. Better let him mess about a bit first before she asked for any money. That was the way to get him proper soft-hearted.

Sitting on the engine Fred slid an arm around her unresisting, but uncomplying, body and tried to draw her to him.

'Watchew want, dear?' she queried plaintively.

'You know.'

He had drawn her to him. Her cheap cloth overcoat and skirt were getting all rucked up. Her legs were getting cold. He rubbed his rough, unshaven cheek along her face. His breath smelt.

'Naughty girl, ain'tcher?'

Blimey, she thought, he's one of them romantic blokes. Ah well, they're better when it comes to paying out. Suppose she had got to play up to him and all.

She put her arm round his neck. He kissed her. Blimey, what a king death. Didn't half pen.

Custom and the knowledge that it was all in the game prevented her from resisting or even stiffening. But he certainly was a clumsy bastard. Some of these lorry sheiks didn't seem to think that a girl might feel cold.

His caresses began to get more insistent. She could feel his heart pounding as she rested her head against his sweat-reeking chest. Now was the time to ask for the drop.

'Going to give me a little present, dear?'

She could feel his body stiffen. None of these bastards liked shelling out any dough. They all thought a girl ought to do it for love. Well, they soon learnt different.

'How much you want?'

She sighed. Same old arguing match all over again.

'How much you got, dear?'

'Give you half a dollar.'

'Don't talk silly, dear. Gimme half a quid.'

'Blimey, you're going from the sublime to the bloody

50

ridiculous.' He had drawn away from her now. She knew she had lost any chance of a ten-shilling drop. Made a mistake she had. Ought to have asked for seven and a sprat. 'Half a quid? You don't half set a high price on your bloody self. Watchew think you are, gold-plated or something?'

'Give us a dollar then, ducks. I'll be nice to you. You won't be sorry.'

'Blimey,' he grumbled, 'and I stood you a couple of teas and a bacon sandwich. And a large Player and all. All right then, all right. If I must I s'pose I must. Here, cop.'

He gave her half a crown, a florin and six-pennorth of coppers.

Impulsively she ran her hand round his neck and drew his face down towards her. He wasn't such a bad bloke after all. She kissed him.

'Come over on this side, dear. It's more comfortable.'

CHAPTER VI

The three detectives sat in the Information Room at Scotland Yard. The chief of them was on the table, swinging his legs as he spoke.

'There you are, you see,' he was saying. 'What did I tell you? Points straight to Mathews. His girl, his dabs. His release from stir corresponds and his pal gives us the tip-off. And now we can't pick him up anywhere. Not even with this.' He tapped the card, with Shorty's description and known habits on it, that he had got from the Criminal Record Office.

'If he hadn't got something to be scared of, he'd be in one of the old hangouts tonight. And he ain't there. The description's been in the evening papers and it's been broadcast twice. Some rat would have grassed him if he'd bin about. He must be hiding, so he must be guilty. Any ideas, anybody?'

His two subordinates were silent. So he turned to the younger of the two with a fatherly smile.

'Well, what've you got to say, Edwards?'

Edwards was one of his special protégés. He thought him a promising young officer and was trying to push him along as fast as he could before promotion got too cluttered up by the young ladies from Hendon College.

'Nothing much, sir.'

'Well, if you was on the run. Where'd you hide?'

'Ooh, I'der, I'd,' Edwards was sycophantically trying to think fast and show the guv'nor what a bright boy he was.

'Yes. I know you'd hide. Point is, where'd you hide?'

Edwards laughed.

'Ha, ha, sir. Damned good. I know what I'd do. I'd take a cheap room somewhere in a quiet district. Clapham Junction, Chalk Farm, Westbourne Park, anywhere like that.'

The chief sighed.

'Use your loaf, Edwards. First, he hadn't any money. We know what he was released with. He can't have copped much, if anything, off the girl. Before he can take even a cheap room he's got to have some luggage. Then the papers have got the description and it's been broadcast. You know what landladies are like. Inquisitive old bitches. If a new lodger come in and he looked at all like what the description sounded she'd've put the squeak in by now. Anyway, if you're right, we'll get him. It's just a matter of time. But I want results quick. They're laughing at us with all these cows getting done in. You got any ideas, Young?'

'Yes, sir. If I was this geezer Mathews, I'd go on the toby.'

'What, as a tramp?' The chief frowned as he considered the idea.

'Well, yes, sir, if necessary.' Young warmed to his task of exposition. Good job if he'd showed this snotty young bastard Edwards up. Proper little bum-crawler. 'But it isn't necessary. Not nowadays. I'd take a jump on a lorry.'

The chief swung his legs more violently and pulled at his lower lip.

'H'm, that's not a bad idea. You're coming on, Young. Well, what'd you do about it?'

'I'd put through a call to all the provincial forces about it, saying that he was expected to be making his way out of the Smoke, lorry-jumping. And I'd ask them to detail all their mobile squads to stop at the transport cafés and make inquiries for any man answering that description, and to instruct all officers who stop either lorries or private cars for any reason to run the rule over the drivers.'

Young paused with a grin. He was out of breath. He could see that the chief was considering what he had said and trying to find fault; but he knew that he had made a good suggestion all the same.

The chief was silent before he spoke.

'Well,' he grudged, 'there's something in what you say. If you're right it would explain why we haven't picked him up in the Smoke. Still, you know what these provincial forces are like. Jealous as hell of us. If they nick a bloke for us we never hear the last of it and there's supposed to be solidarity and teamwork among policemen, too,' he said bitterly. 'Still, I'll try your idea, for what it's worth. Have the call put out, Edwards.'

'Yes, sir.'

Edwards sprang up to do the guv'nor's bidding, but he was stopped by a wave of the hand.

'Just a minute. Put the call out to our Mobile Metropolitan patrols and all. He must have picked up a lift somewhere near London if he got one at all. Tell them to inquire at likely cafés and filling stations. Okay. That's all. Now, Young. Have you got that list of pawn-brokers and jewellers you went to today, checking up on them snide sovereigns? Let's go over it and see what you've done.'

'Yes, sir. Here it is.'

Radiantly Young produced the papers. He had done a good job on this, too, he knew. Getting into the guv'nor's good books, that's what he was doing.

For half an hour or more they checked over the papers. When they had finished the guv'nor unbent.

'Well done, Young. You done a good job there, son. I reckon we've got just about enough evidence to convict on here. You better go down to the local station, ask the DDI for a couple of officers and go and nick the bastard. Give him a good coating in the station. He'll come his guts all right. He ought to cop out for five or seven stretch for this little job. I suppose you want to handle this case in court yourself.'

'Well, er, yes sir, if I may.'

'Okay, okay. Well, get busy now. Yes, what is it?'

A clerk came up to him with a radio message from a mobile patrol attached to S Division.

'Blimey, Young. You was right here and all. Looks like it anyhow. A man answering the description of Albert Mathews got a lift from a driver at a café on the Great North. Driver's name unknown. Lorry's number unknown. H'm, that means his mates don't want to drop the bloke into it for giving lifts. Lorry known to be proceeding north. Belongs to Aberdonian Transit.

'Here. Get hold of a blower quick. Call up this Aberdonian Transit if they're still open. Get the number or numbers of any of their lorries going north and the probable route. We'll get the bastard.'

Young hurried to the telephone. He came back disconsolately shaking his head.

'Bleeding place closed, sir,' he said.

'Been a time finding that lot out.'

'I put a call through to a pal o' mine in the motor trade. Asked him about Aberdonian. It's a Glasgow firm and its lorries travel on this route.' He consulted a piece of paper. 'London, Welwyn, Biggleswade, Stamford, Grantham, Doncaster, Wetherby, Boroughbridge, Richmond, Carlisle, Glasgow.'

'Good. That's fine. You used your nut there. Let's have a look.'

He grabbed the piece of paper. 'Can't be much further than Stamford now. That's what? Lincoln, ain't it, or has it got a force of its own? Blimey. Never mind. Find out all the forces between Stamford and Carlisle and tell them to stop any north-bound Aberdonian lorry and to detain any passenger. Any excuse'll do. Suspected person, no; can't have that. Tell them to use their nuts. Detain, mind you, not arrest. Hurry now.'

CHAPTER VII

The road stretched on endlessly northwards. With his coat collar turned up and his hands deep in his pockets, Shorty had shivered as the wind had whistled and blown through the glassless window of the cab across the flat fields of Middlesex, Bedfordshire, Huntingdonshire. Occasionally on his left a row of lights had shown where a town lay. Once, running parallel to a railway line, they had been overtaken by the roar and lights of a train. Alf had said nothing except to curse every now and then at the lights of a passing private driver. The noise from the central engine of the Leyland made all talk impossible.

Sometimes Shorty amused himself by looking at the roadside signs which the lorry's headlights lighted up as they passed. 'This is a Franco sign.' Blimey, they didn't want to let the Communists see that. There had been that bloke back in the nick who'd been a Communist and he didn't half carry on about Franco. Fancy a Spanish general sticking road signs up all over England. Sauce.

Another sign was in the form of a ship and advertised cruises to the Sunny Mediterranean. Bit of all right to be there instead of freezing to death along the Great North Road. Jammy. Right out of the way from English coppers. Lucky touch if he got a job on a ship. Now, there was an idea. Beat it from Doncaster to Liverpool. They couldn't be far away from each other. Both up north anyway, and get a job going away to sea. Not much chance of that though. Plenty of seamen on the ribs. Everybody was on the ribs nowadays. Everybody and everything.

Earlier on the ride had not been so bad. At first they

had passed a bunch of roadhouses. All gaily lighted up and with sounds of music coming out of them, so that Shorty had been able to amuse himself by feeling envious. Even in the villages there had been lights in the windows and people walking around in the streets and the cheerful red glow from behind the blinds in the still-open boozers. But now the pubs were all closed, the villages were miles apart and then they were only long streets of sleeping houses. There were, it was true, occasional cafés with laden lorries standing outside by the petrol pumps with the patience that carriers' horses had once stood outside the inns by the horse troughs.

Alf did not seem to want to stop. He roared on through the night. Onwards, onwards, onwards, sitting bolt upright in his cab with his pale face set and his eyes fixed on the road. Shorty amused himself by counting the strips of white paint that marked the centre of the road.

One, two, three, four, five, six, seven. One, two, three, four, five, six, seven. One, two, three, four, five, six, seven. They seemed to dart down the road to disappear underneath the oncoming lorry. One, two, three, four, five, six, seven. Hallo. He was slowing down. Christ, don't say he was going to stop. Perhaps there was a caff ahead and there was going to be a chance of copping a cup of tea.

Gaw blimey. It was only a level crossing that he was slowing down for.

Alf leant over and volunteered practically his first remark since they had started.

'Ought to do away with these bleeders. Reglar death traps.'

'Ar.'

One, two, three, four, five, six, seven. One, two, three, four, five, six, seven. Counting white lines again, trying to fill in the time. Why, blimey, this was as bad as being in stir. He'd acted right berkish. If on'y he'd of kept his head everything would have been all right. He didn't ought to have tried to kid the old dear. He ought to have gone straight to the cops and come his guts. Now he'd been and messed it up proper and no mistake. If only. Bleeding hell, where was the sense in saying if only. Regretting didn't get you nowhere at all.

That bloke, what was his name – Charley – back at the caff had been right. A lot of blokes didn't know when they were well-off.

A kind of nostalgia for his cell filled him.

Well, it was warm in there anyway and when you'd done the first fourteen days and they'd let you have a mattress it wasn't so bad. A bloke could curl up under his blankets and snore at night peacefully and be miles from anywhere. And they couldn't pin any murders on you that you hadn't done.

They roared through a little town. In the market square, across from the church was a brightly-lit little café. It looked cosy. Shorty leant across the engine and shouted.

'Where's this dump?'

'Stamford. Going to stop soon.'

The dreary scenery of Lincolnshire and Rutland succeeded that of Northampton. Shorty began to feel sick. He tried to keep his eyes off the road. Staring at the white lines made him feel worse. Alf stopped the lorry by a café. Like a flash Shorty leapt down and staggered on numbed legs across to the petrol pumps where he relieved nature. Once he had tried to do so on the road, opening the cab door, but it had been too cold. Alf looked at the knots on the load, at the petrol gauge and at the tyres before he followed Shorty's example. Then he said:

'Let's go and have a cup of ackermaracker,' leading the way across to the café.

''Tain't half cold,' said Shorty.

'Not half. You must be bleeding perished in them clothes and all. You ain't dressed right for the road. Look at me.'

Alf was wearing an old overcoat and a short London bus driver's coat underneath, which he had bought through the Saturday bargain page in the *Daily Express*, grey flannel trousers, a high-neck sweater, a shirt, a woollen scarf, woollen underpants and vest, grey woollen army socks and ankle boots.

'You ain't got no overcoat or nothing. You must be bloody dead.'

Shorty went up to the counter and planked down three-pence.

'Two cups of tea, mate.'

'Fourpence, please,' said the man behind the bar. 'Tuppence a cup here.'

Shorty looked at Alf with raised, inquiring eyebrows.

Alf answered: 'Yus, mate. 'S right. Puts it up ha'penny a cup after midnight.'

'After midnight, is it? Blimey. No bloody wonder I feel tired.' He rubbed his puffy eyes.

''Ark at her,' said Alf, pouring out some tea into his saucer and blowing on it noisily.

'Coppers ain't half bin active tonight,' said the counterman conversationally. 'There been two mobile patrols in here having a look round like.'

Shorty hastily looked at a road map that was hanging on the wall so as to hide his expression. The blood had drained from his cheeks, leaving them white, and then rushed back again. He knew that even the tips of his ears were red. His scalp was tingling under his hat. Well, if his face was red let's hope they'd put it down to the heat in the café after being out there in the bleeding cold.

'Yeah?' said Alf, lighting a fag. 'What'd they want?'

Shorty, his ears pricked up, looked somewhere across towards Bristol for Grantham.

'Dunno. After some poor bastard. Hadn't got no photographs to show me though like when they was looking for that other bloke that time.'

The conversation lapsed. Alf looked across towards Shorty.

'Going to have a bit 'o cake or something to eat, chum?'

'Don't mind if I do. I could go something. What they got?'

Shorty, the moment of danger past, strolled across to the counter. Alf had taken out a bundle of log sheets and wetted the tip of his pencil with his tongue.

'That apple pie looks all right,' said Shorty. 'I'll have a bit of that.'

Alf glanced at the glass dish.

'Yeah. I'll have a bit and all. How much, mate?'

'Fourpence to you, chum.'

Alf passed over the coppers and bent to his log sheets again. Shorty watched him for a bit.

Blimey, nobody could say he'd got a talkative bastard for a mate. Come all this bleeding way they had and he'd hardly said a blind word. Very nigh as bad as being in stir.

'Them forms,' he said, 'must be a bit of a puzzle.'

'It's a bit of a puzzler, thinking out bleeding lies and fiddling them to make them come right.'

'What they all about?'

'Werl, you see,' Alf took a bite of apple pie and a good mouthful of tea. He had, he knew, quite a long speech ahead of him. 'It's police regulations. Under the new Act you got to fill them in and the cops are entitled to take a look at the bastards any time they feel like it. You see, you ain't supposed to drive more'n eleven hours at a stretch plus an hour for your dinner. That's twelve hours in all. Take the Aberdeen trip now. Aberdeen's a tidy way from the Smoke and the firm I'm on gives a week for the job. Up there, unload, reload, come down. You try to sort that out, chum. You ain't allowed to drive more'n eleven hours' driving time without an eight-hour break. Takes a bit of bleeding doing.'

'I should cocoa.'

'Yerce. You'd be surprised and if I stop off for a cup of tea or something o' that sort that's part of me eleven hours' driving time wasted. If I make twenty-five miles an hour with my lot I'm bleeding lucky and I reckon I'm entitled to a cup o' tea and a smoke. I reckon if I didn't fiddle me log sheets I'd only go something like hundred and eighty or two hundred miles to me eleven hours. This here Glasgow trip they give me five days. All in all that's hundred and twenty hours' driving time. Work that out.'

'Yerce. Must be a proper bastard.'

'You're right there, mate. Too bloody true it's a bastard. If it wasn't that you didn't have a guv'nor with you all the time nobody wouldn't be a lorry driver. Scum of the frog and toad, that's the way we're treated. One breach of the Act, smallest bloody breach and we're nicked. Very hot on us the police.'

'Your firm pay the fines and all?'

'Garn, don't make me laugh. You're talking silly. My firm? Blimey.'

'Well,' Shorty defended. 'Some firms do.'

'Mister, my firm's a Scotch firm. Yus, I pay the fines out of me enormous wages of two pun ten a week, with half a quid bonus for a Glasgow trip and fourteen and a tanner for Aberdeen. 'Nother thing. Look at the way the private drivers treat us. Rank bad bloody drivers all of them. Not got a ha'porth of bloody consideration. Drive all over the road, never dim their lights, and if a lorry driver and a private car gets in trouble, who's to blame? The poor bloody lorry driver. You can stake your life on that.'

'But all these forms and regulations and that must have given you a bit of help, ain't they?'

'Blimey, mate. You don't know what you're talking about. Just messing us about, that's all they're doing, messing us about. Before this Act come into force I could do me trip in me own time, stop when I liked and as I liked. If it came on to rain and the roads was a bit skiddy I'd take a couple of hours off. Take a tart to the pictures if there was one in a town I was passing through that I knew. So long as I done the trip in the time they'd laid down the firm didn't have a dicky bird to say. Now I'm messed and bitched about from pillar to bloody post. The blokes this Act would have done a bit of good to are London blokes driving delivery wagons and for the sand and ballast firms and all that caper. Those poor bastards sometimes put in up to fifteen and sixteen hours a day and they don't come under the Act, neither.'

'Yerce, there's some bastard thing wrong with every job,' said Shorty with his mouth full of apple pie. 'How many nights d'you get at home in a week?'

'Werl, that depends. I brought a load down this morning, kipped at home this afternoon and I'm off up north again. If I get home round about the weekend I may touch lucky for a couple of nights. Some single blokes ain't got no homes. They just kip in kip houses. 'Tain't really a job for a married man this. Come on, we got to get going.'

Reluctantly Shorty followed him out. Alf started the engine, but before he drove off, he leant across and spoke to Shorty. His voice showed that he was a bit scared.

'Look here, mate, I don't like what the geezer was saying about the police,' he began and Shorty's heart began to hammer again. 'If they're after some bloke they might start stopping all the transport and then I'd be in a nice mess. I ain't supposed to give lifts. So you better say you work for the firm and all – Aberdonian Transit. Spin them a fanny. Use your loaf. Say I'm taking you up to Glasgow so as you can bring another wagon down. That'll do. They're short of a driver up there, see?'

'Okay, mate. I get you.'

Blimey, thought Shorty as they started off again. I'm for it this time. Drop the other poor bastard in for it and all. More of them lines on the road. One, two, three, four, five, six, seven. They weren't likely to pull up lorries on the road, surely. Make a round of the caffs, maybe, but that was all. Blimey, it certainly was cold. Poor bloody Alice she was cold and all. Laid out on a mortuary slab. Caw. They'd be having an inquest on her tomorrow the prying sons of bitches. What'd it got to do with them. When the poor kid was alive they hadn't bloody well bothered their heads about her except to knock her off every now and then and do her for soliciting. One, two, three, four, five, six, seven, eight. Counted one more that time. If the sweeny car did stop for running the rule over the lorry what was the best thing? Cut and run for it? Blimey no. Try to fanny it out the way this bloke had said. They might be after something else. Strike a light they had boys on the crooked lark up this way and all, didn't they? How'd they have picked up his trail so quick.

Nevertheless every time Shorty saw the lights of a private car coming towards him he nearly stopped breathing. His fists were clenched in the side pockets of his coat and he had picked at the quick of his thumbs until they were bleeding. He shivered and fidgeted so much that Alf found him getting on his nerves. He leant over and yelled at him.

'What's up, mate? Cold or something?'

'Not half,' Shorty roared back with chattering teeth.

'Soon be in Doncaster and you'll be able to get a kip there.'

'What's that town we just run through?'

'Newark.'

It was coming on to rain heavily. On Alf's side of the cab the windscreen wiper was working merrily, but in spite of the cold, the steam on the inside was such that every now and then he had to wipe the glass with his coat sleeve. He was swearing steadily as he drove. Shorty, who could see nothing ahead of him, had resigned himself to cold, discomfort and a probable arrest. He leant back and stuck out his feet. They touched something soft.

Blimey, an old sack. What luck.

He leant down, picked it up and wrapped it round his knees, tucking it in carefully at either side. Well, there was a slice of cake for you. It certainly made a difference. Having quite a comfortable ride now he was.

He felt in his pocket and found a cigarette end which he lit.

Caw, there were worse things than riding in lorries. What was he to do in Doncaster? If the squeak was in, he dursn't go to a kip house. The best thing would be to go to a caff, trust to luck on getting a quick lift out of it before he was nailed, and . . .

A car rushed past them. Shorty could see 'Police' glittering on its front in lighted letters. He held his breath. Alf drove the slow ponderous lorry onwards. Shorty looked out in the mirror that hung at his side as well as Alf's. He could see the car turning round. His throat went dry.

Blimey. What was he to do. Cut out and run for it. No. Use your loaf. Think fast, son. Think fast.

The police car was behind them, gonging. Shorty sat with every muscle taut. He was biting his lip. Trickles of sweat ran down from under his hat. Alf sighed and drew into the side of the road.

The sweenies drew up alongside. Four men got out of the car, one going to Shorty's side of the cab, the other three to Alf's. Three of them were in uniform.

'You work for Aberdonian Transit Company, lad?' said the non-uniformed man.

'Yes, that's right,' said Alf.

'Pick this bloke up at a caff in St Albans, didn't you?'

'No, I picked him up at our yards in Southwark.'

'That true?' one of them asked Shorty.

'Course it's true.'

'What were you doing around there?'

'I work for the firm and all. He's giving me a ride up to Glasgow. I've got to bring another lorry down south.'

'Yeah? Got a licence?'

'Sure.'

'Let's have a look.'

One of Alf's guardians came round and stood on the grass verge near Shorty's side of the cab. Shorty felt in all his pockets. Well, he had to play for time, didn't he?

'Must have left it in me overcoat.' He could delay no longer.

'Where's that?'

'I made a mistake and left it in the caff at St Albans where I was having something to eat.'

'Oh yeah? Left your coat behind on a night like this. Don't come that old acid. We wasn't born yesterday. Think I've just come up? Hop down off the wagon and let's take a look at you. You and all driver.'

Shorty clambered down. A policeman put out his arm, not to help him but to prevent him trying to run for it.

'Come over here the both of you in front of the head-lights and let's take a look at you.'

Alf sighed and obeyed. Shorty, with stiffened limbs and sickened heart, went over in front of the lorry. The head-lights from the two vehicles made a nice patch of light. It was raining hard and in the cones of light the raindrops showed up prettily. A lorry lumbered past them on its journey south, the driver sticking his head out of the window and looking curiously at the group.

The plain-clothes copper spoke to Shorty in wearied tones.

'Ain't got no sense some of you people. Just come out

of Pentonville Prison and you have to go and get yourself in another mess.'

Shorty repressed a start. They'd got him dead to rights. Alf looked at him curiously and then began to protest.

''Ere. Watchew want me for? I ain't done nothing. Honest working-man, that's me. I'll get all behind in me trip if you keep me messing about like this.'

'Watchew want to tell me lies for? You didn't pick this bloke up in Southwark, did you?'

'N-no.'

'Well then. You keep quiet. How'd I know you ain't been aiding and abetting. There's a law against harbouring fugitives. Let's have a look at you,' he was speaking to Shorty. 'How tall are you?'

'Dunno.'

'You go about five five. Blue suit, white shirt, brown and red tie, dark brown hair, grey eyes. S'pose there's no use arsting you if your name's Mathews, is there?'

''Tain't, so there.'

'What is it then?'

'Allen.' Shorty said the first name that came into his head.

'Don't talk soft. They hanged him this morning, same as they're going to do with you.'

'Yeah?' Shorty was thinking fast and clearly. His feet were wet through standing in a pool of water that had collected in a bad patch of road. 'So you're charging me with murder now?'

'No. We just want to have a little talk with you.'

'Well, you got to charge me and caution me first. Blimey, you provincial coppers don't know your own business.'

'You ought to know all about it. You been in enough times.'

'Here,' Alf chimed in, 'if you want to have a little talk,

can't you have it some other place? I'm getting bleeding wet. 'Tain't half coming down.'

With one accord three of the policemen turned on him fiercely.

'Shut up you.'

'That's enough from you.'

'We'll be putting you somewhere you don't want to be.'

The grip on Shorty's arm was loosened. He shook himself free and ran for the hedge. It was slippery on the grass, but he was more nimble than the fourteen-stone policemen who ran behind him. Scrambling through the prickly hedge, he landed on his hands and knees in the ploughed field. He could hear the policemen shouting.

'Here, Stan, quick. There's a gate down there. Come on. Put a jerk in it.'

He picked himself up and started to run. The heavy soil clung about his shoes and every now and again he stumbled across a furrow and fell on to his face. His heart felt as if it was going to burst.

The sounds of pursuit grew fainter and more distant.

CHAPTER VIII

Shorty ran across the field until he felt that he was going to drop dead. His heart was pounding like a sledge-hammer. His hat blew off early in the race, but he was unconscious of the wind and the rain that were batting against the right side of his body. Little spots danced in front of his desperate eyes and phlegm and saliva were spattered across his muddy face. Earth clung to the soles of his flimsy shoes, earth had seeped in over the top of them. His hands were bleeding from the briars and wire of the hedge through which he had scrambled.

He paused and looked behind him. It was pitch dark and he could hear no sounds of pursuit, not even any shouts.

Blimey, he was in a state now. Miles out in the bloody country. He'd get lost as like as not if he didn't watch out. The thing to look out for was that he mustn't run back to the road whatever he did. People ran round in circles when they were lost.

Fragments of adventure stories that he had read in tuppenny bloods when he had been a little spiv in Kilburn raced through his mind as he set off again. Right ahead of him was a light shining in a house. If he made for that he ought to be all right.

Crash! He fell on his face again and lay there for a moment on the cool earth with the taste of mud in his mouth. Then he got up again and staggered on. His legs felt like lead and he could run no more. He stumbled again, recovered and went on at a walking pace. The slops must be shaken off by now.

The light in the house had vanished. He could see it nowhere. Either he was facing a completely different direction or it had gone out. He suddenly became conscious of the pain in his scratched hands. Before he could save himself he had stepped into a brook. He reached out with one foot and found it was dry land.

Well, that was okay, anyway. He could not have gone back on his tracks. That had been the first brook he had crossed. Onwards, ever onwards he stumbled and tripped through a field of roots. Once or twice he put up a bird that flew away with a startled whirring of its wings.

What the hell was he going to do now? A London bloke was done for in the bloody country. Blimey. It wasn't half a turn-out. Well, take it as it comes. It was all in the game. No sense in crossing your bridges until you came to them.

He halted.

Out of the blinding darkness in front of him came the sound of voices; came little stabs of light. It was blokes with flashlights.

He dropped prone on his face and lay there with beating heart.

All that bloody running and misery for nothing. He was done for now.

Neither the voices nor the lights seemed to come any nearer. He strained his red-rimmed tired eyes trying to see through the darkness.

If the lights weren't coming no nearer they must be standing waiting for him. There must be a lane somewhere and they were there. He couldn't see coppers in a field if they could help it.

He counted the lights. One, two, three. Scattered. About forty foot between them. They must have left one slop guarding the other poor bastard. Well, he wouldn't be giving no lifts again in a hurry. Best thing to do was to crawl forward towards the lights and try and make out what was happening. At any rate he might be able to sort out what they were saying. Have a go anyway.

He went forward cautiously on hands and knees. The lights were wavering from left to right. They made it all the darker. His ears magnified every sound that he made. The rustling of the swede tops were to him like thunderbolts. He paused, trying to pick out what their voices were saying, but the only noise he could hear was the lonely whine of the wind in the telegraph wires.

Wires!

There must be a proper road there and all.

He lay flat on his face again and tried to listen.

Again the whining of the wind was all he heard. Then a voice complaining:

'Wasting our time, standing around here in the rain, that's what we're doing. How'd we know he's coming this way?'

'If he's got into this bloody field he's got to come out. I'm not going to let the bastard slip through my fingers as easy as this.'

'Well, he ain't bound to come out this way. He might have doubled back. Crafty as a fox, that's what he is.'

'Well, if he'd doubled back, Stan'd 've got him. He's over there with the lorry driver. Just a question of time, that's all.'

'Gaw blimey O'Reilly, Sarge,' a third voice joined in, 'don't go saying we've got to wait here till dawn and we can see him. Let's string out like a line of beaters and pick him up.'

'Yerce. You want him to slip through our fingers, that's what you want. Listen, we come down that turning to the left in the car, then we turned left again. He was running straight across the fields. He's bound to come right into our arms.'

Oh oh, thought Shorty, so they came down a turning to

the left, did they? Well, that means there's a lane or a road or something on me right. That's handy to know anyway.

The first voice was speaking again.

'How we to know he kept on running straight? Blokes do funny things in the dark. He might 've gone off to the right and crossed that other turning. He might 've gone off to the left and be away over the fields over there. We're looking bleeding silly, if you arst me, standing here watching out for a bloke who might be three mile away or something.'

'Ar. Well, there's something in that all said and done. Reckon he's bin and gone and give us the slip, don't you, Sarge?'

'No. We'll wait a bit yet. Wait a bit. Oy, what's that?'

Shorty had made an incautious rustle. The sergeant ran his torch up and down.

'You're seeing things, Sarge.'

'All right, I'm seeing things. But, mark me words, young feller, that bloke's in this here field somewhere. Here I tell you what. Run up the road and turn the car headlights on to the field.'

A light went out and there came the sound of heavy boots squelching up a wet road, a sound like somebody chewing a lump of sugar.

Now was his chance. If he dived off to the right now he might make a getaway. Cautiously he slithered a little in a crabwise motion.

'There,' yelled the sergeant. 'What's that? Someone's moving around.'

He swung his torch in the wrong direction. Shorty slithered again, got into a crouching position and ran a few steps to the right. Both policemen's torches were flashing about in the darkness. Shorty ran to the hedge. He was well to the right of both of them. He was on the grass border now and his sounds were deadened. Bending down so that he was covered by the hedge he ran. He was level with the crunching footsteps. He was ahead of them.

The policeman, away from the sergeant, was taking advantage of his opportunity to have a smoke by halting to light a cigarette. Shorty came to a five-barred gate. He peered through it. Slightly ahead of him and to the left was the police car. He could see the side lamps.

Okay. He had made his plan. If he didn't think quickly now, if his plan came unstuck, he was nailed and he could gamble on these flatties giving him a damned good hiding in return for the dance he had led them. Hurriedly he looked for a weapon. A good stick would do fine. He felt on the ground, in the hedge. There was nothing handy.

Ah well. He must do without. Just trust to luck and surprise.

Still half-covered by the hedge, he mounted on to the gate and crouched there ready to spring. The policeman sauntered up, his left hand covering the glow from his cigarette, whistling.

Shorty leapt. Even his light weight caught the big man by surprise. They fell to the ground with Shorty on top. The little man was on his feet. Three well-directed kicks, the fruits of the lessons learnt in many a London street fight, put the copper out. One to the crutch, one to the solar plexus, one to the face. He grunted three times and lay still. Shorty dashed for the car. It was grand to be running on a road.

'There he goes!'

He heard the sergeant's voice as he jumped into the car. He slammed the gears into reverse and backed down the road. It was a hell of a time since he had driven a jam-jar anyway. When the roads met he swung back to his right and then down to meet the main road. There was no sense in letting himself get tied up in these back doubles. A bloke never knew where he was likely to end up.

When he was out on the main road, he turned left-handed and drove north. With a laugh he let the car rip out as fast as it would go. Well, he was making the old sweeny car as muddy as hell and he'd left four bloody coppers nicely stranded in the country on a lousy wet night.

Even if they did top him, he had done something good anyway.

CHAPTER IX

Reg smirked at Molly as she came up to the counter. He did not see many tarts in the cafés now since the police had taken to driving the lorry girls off the Great North Road.

'Yes, sweetness, what can I do for you?'

She smiled a weary smile at him. Blimey, she was tired.

'Gimme a cup of tea. No sugar.'

'Sweet enough, already?'

'S'right.'

She sank down into the creaking wicker armchair. Fred had dropped her off in Newark. In a café there she had picked up a private driver who had given her seventeen and six. She was all in. Carlisle to Coventry. Coventry to Newark. Newark northwards. Join the lorry girls and see England by night. Reg made her tea. He put it on the counter near her chair with a bang that shot some of the tea out of the cup into the saucer.

'One smashing cup of Rosy Lee for the little lady.'

Molly yawned. This mug gave her a pain. Didn't half think he was a sheik.

'Any chance of any transport tonight, sonny boy?'

'Yerce later. There's all the milk lorries in about half-hour.'

Molly got up. She put a penny in the diddler machine and pulled down the handle. Two threes and a nought. She copped twopence. Leaving the two pennies down in the cup, she fed another coin into the machine. Nought one nought. She picked up her winnings, put them into her bag and went and sat down again. Won twopence. No, she hadn't. She'd lost twopence to win twopence. That's what took the mugs in.

Wearily she took her tea and stirred it.

The next town she got to, she'd go to kip. Get a driver to give her a lift somewhere and go to kip. Have a snooze. That's what. She leant back in her chair and yawned, showing her discoloured teeth. They let kips here and all. P'raps she'd take one here if they had rooms and not dormitories. Kip. You can't beat it.

She yawned again and nodded forward in the wicker chair.

Reg got bored. Uninteresting bloody pusher this. Didn't have much to say for herself.

He started stacking cups in the sink preparatory to washing them up. Plates stained with egg, knives, forks, spoons. Into the swill tub he threw all the bacon rind, bits of bread, and skins of fish. The guv'nor got good money flogging all that junk to a local farmer. He nipped his cigarette and stuck it behind his ear. He looked at the frying pan. Not much sense in washing that. There was a lot of nice fat in it and they'd be wanting their breakfasts soon. Ah well. He sighed. Better get stuck into it.

He turned on the hot tap. The gas in the water heater leapt into life and the hot water gushed into the sink. He picked up a packet of soapflakes and dosed the water liberally. No sense in being close over them. They didn't half help the washing up and the guv'nor had got plenty of money to play with. He wouldn't miss a few soapflakes.

The door opened, letting an icy draught into the smelly room. Molly looked up. Reg turned his head. A muddied man came in. He was hatless and soaked through, panting and out of breath. Hurriedly he closed the door and then went up to the counter. Molly looked at him curiously. There was a long tear in one side of his dirty trousers.

'Cup o' tea, mate, and a bacon sandwich.'

'There you are, you see,' said Reg to himself triumphantly. 'If I'd 've washed the frying pan, where'd I've bin?'

Aloud he said: 'Just a minute mate.'

The man went over to the oil stove and held out his hands to its grateful warmth. He darted little glances around the room. Suddenly his eyes rested on Molly's face. He went over to her.

'Ain't you Molly?' he said.

She nodded.

'Remember me?'

She shook her head.

'Can't say I do.'

'Remember the old caff in the Edgware Road?'

'Yerce.' Her voice was still doubtful.

'Doncher remember the boys that used to get in there?'

'Yerce.'

'Garn. You're sprucing. You got me figured out and weighed up.'

There was menace in his tone. He was forbidding her to forget him, daring her to remember him.

'Straight I don't. No kidding.'

Reg turned away from the stove and watched them curiously. This bloke looked like starting trouble.

'Go on,' his voice had sunk to a whisper. 'You remember Shorty. Shorty Mathews.'

'Blige me. Course I do.' She laughed shrilly. Her voice took on a higher pitch. 'The bloke that used to go with Alice. Alice Carson.'

'Shut up.' He was hissing like a stage villain. 'Don't go shouting it out all over the place.'

He sat down on a stool near Molly and, running his forearm over his forehead, opened his mouth to speak. It was obvious that the effort had cost him a lot of willpower.

'Here, mister,' Reg hollered out, 'your order's ready.'

'Okay.'

Shorty went up to the counter, collected his stuff and then went back and sat down by Molly again. He stuffed his mouth full, took a big gulp of tea and then started to talk.

'Listen, Kid,' he said quietly. 'Give us a handout, will you? I'm in a right two and eight.'

'What's up?'

'What's up? Plenty! I'm on the run. Look, will you do something for me? Next stop's Doncaster, ain't it? Okay. Well, I got a car outside, I'll give you a lift in there. I'll lie doggo in a café or somewhere while you go to a hotel and book a room. Say your husband's been held up by engine trouble in his car and that he's at the garage. Then come back and fetch me. Okay? I got to have a rest. I ain't had no kip.'

'Me neither.'

'And I bin chased across miles of bloody fields. Look at me.'

'Yerce, you look like Gandhi or something. All right, I'll do it.'

'That's the kid. Come on. I don't want to waste time.'

He gulped down the rest of the tea and they went out to the car. Molly sat down in the front seat.

'Blimey,' she said, 'where'd you get this?'

'Knocked it off. Police car.' He was driving with his foot rammed down on the accelerator.

'Caw. That's a stroke to come out with. Where's your luggage?'

'Ain't got none.'

'Well, use your loaf. They won't let you into no hotel at this time of the morning except you've got some luggage, covered in mud and all.'

'Yerce. There's something in that. Well, I'll have to get some, that's all.'

'How?'

'Do a screwing job.'

'Oy nark it. I don't want to get mixed up in no screwing jobs.'

'You don't have to, baby. Leave it to me. All you got to do is to sit in the car and wait. There ought to be some easy gaffs out here in the country.'

He drove more slowly. Away on the left was another side turning. He took it.

'Oy, where going? This don't lead to Doncaster.'

'All right, all right. I know. I don't want to do no jobs on the main road though. There's bound to be a house somewhere around here.'

And sure enough there was. It was a tall red-brick villa standing, as house agents say, in its own grounds. Shorty drove past it, stopped the car and switched out all the lights. He put one hand on Molly's.

'Listen, Kid, you sit here and keep quiet. You'll be all right. If I come unstuck, pretend you know nothing about it. Just put in the gee. Say that I told you I wanted to get out of the car for a minute. So long. Wish me luck. Keep the engine running.'

He kissed her on the mouth and, leaving the car, tip-toed back to the gate of the house. For a moment he stood by the gatepost, looking up the drive with pursed lips. It ought to be easy. He clambered over the gate, it was quieter than opening it, and walked on the flower-beds so as to avoid stepping on the gravel. At the back of the house there was, as he expected, a glass-roofed veranda outside the drawing room. He would have to be very clever to do that without any tools and without making a noise, so he walked round to the kitchens. Ah! As usual, a window whose catch had not been closed. He stood there for a minute to draw breath and get possession of himself.

Unlike most jobs that he had gone on, this time he was

not scared at all. A calm contentment filled him. He was just a workman doing a job of work.

Carefully and slowly he pulled down a sash. A dog barked. Yappy little bastard, oh hell. He pulled down the sash a little farther. The dog went on barking. It was inside the house. He got through the window and landed on the kitchen table. The cloth slipped and he slithered off to land on the floor with a bang. The dog set up a furious barking. He heard footsteps on the landing upstairs as he lay there on the floor with barked skins and banged head. Voices.

'Shut up, Peter! Lay down. Bad dog!'

'Go downstairs and see if there was anything, Will,' a woman's voice said. 'I did hear a noise, I'm sure.'

Shorty held his breath and lay still. It was the only thing to do. Will was certain to be too scared to come down. For what seemed like ages he lay there with the cold flags of the kitchen floor caressing his cheeks. The little dog stopped yapping. He could hear its master soothing it. The voices died away. He heard the floorboards creak, the bed-springs groan. It was time to get to work again.

He struck a match with the flame guarded by the palm of his hand. The momentary light was enough to give him the layout of the kitchen. He slipped off his shoes and in his muddied socks padded across the room, with his hands held out in front of him, like a sleepwalker. His out-stretched fingers touched the smoothness of the painted wall and he waved his hands like a hypnotist.

Well, he'd left enough dabs on the window to let them know the job was his and the bogeys wouldn't come examining all the walls.

At last he located the woodwork and the icy touch of the metal of the door catch. Good. They'd never locked it. Carefully he turned the handle, carefully and gradually opened the door. It creaked.

'Shut up, Peter. Be quiet!'

The dog's barking subsided into muttered growls. Shorty had opened the door wide enough for him to squeeze through into a kind of lobby. He struck another match. There were four doors. They were all closed except for that leading on to the kitchen. There was no window, no skylight. Good. He fumbled on the wall and found an electric switch.

The brilliance of the light dazzled him and he had to stand stock-still, shading his eyes with his hand, and then he was able to take in the full grandeur of the scene. There were overcoats in profusion, a nice gold-mounted umbrella and a bag of golf clubs, which would help to put up a nice front at the hotel.

Blimey, talk about all modern conveniences! On the green baize-covered table, next to a fern in a china pot, lay a neat little electric torch. Well, if that wasn't handy, what was?

He looked around at the doors. One looked suspiciously like a cupboard under the stairs and such a cupboard very frequently held a suitcase. He opened the cupboard and shone his torch inside.

Blimey, yes, a nice little peter, too. This was all working out too good to be true.

He dragged out the suitcase, helped himself to three bottles of whisky that he found there and put them inside the case which he laid on the table beside the golf clubs and an overcoat which he had chosen.

He stood upright and scratched his muddy head.

A wise man would scarper how. He had what he wanted. Well, it seemed a pity to go and leave a job half done. There might be some ready lob.

He put on the overcoat, a bowler hat that was too large for him and made his ears stick out like Clark Gable's, slung the golf clubs round his body and, picking up the suitcase, strutted out into the hall. He shone his torch around. Two doors. One meant the dining room, the other the living room. A leather shopping bag lay on a table. He stepped across towards it. As he stepped his golf clubs rattled.

Aw, nuts to that dog barking!

He picked up the bag and felt inside. A ball of wool, some knitting, two knitting needles, a book of shiny paper, and a purse. A half-quid note and a handful of silver inside. He stuffed the money in his pocket. Not much, but better than nothing.

Caw, yes. That'd be a good giggle.

He tied a couple of strands of wool across the foot of the stairs, tying the ends round the newel posts.

Won't half come a bleeding tumble when he comes down. The dog was barking more furiously than ever when he went into the dining room. He looked around.

Nothing much.

He bit into an apple, and cracked a couple of walnuts. One of them was bad, so he threw the shells on to the floor and took a bite out of another apple.

Blimey, there were sounds upstairs. Steps again. Voices.

'There *is* somebody downstairs, Will. Peter wouldn't carry on barking like this. You and Frank go on down.'

He laid his suitcase on the ground and put on his shoes again. A bloke couldn't get away barefoot. That was stone ginger.

He opened one of the dining-room windows so as to fix himself a getaway and then stood by the door looking out into the hall. With his mouth still half-full of apple, he made a grotesque figure with a muddy face, an outsized bowler hat, an overcoat that reached half-way down his legs, golf clubs and a suitcase.

Interestedly he peered round the door. A light went on upstairs. Lots of footsteps came down the corridor. The dog was having hysterics.

It was high time that he was out of it.

He rushed to the open window and swung his legs through. The golf clubs caught against the pane and pulled him back. He made another effort and landed flat on his face on a flower-bed. Simultaneously there was an awful crash in the hall.

He caught hold of something to help himself up. It was a rose bush, and he tore his hands again. Still, he was on his feet and racing for the gate.

Before his pursuers had got the front door open he was in the car.

'Quick, Kid, I was bleeding nigh nailed.'

He slung the suitcase into the back seat and drove off.

'That's not the way to Doncaster.'

'Can't help that. I got to get away. Dursn't turn round.'

He drove on until he came to a crossroads.

'What's on the signpost?'

Molly stuck her head out of the car window and looked. She closed her eyes and yawned.

Blimey. She was tired. The sooner she got to that hotel and went to kip the better.

'Come on, put a bit of jildy into it. I ain't got all day.'

'Nottingham, Leicester to the left,' Molly read, still yawning. 'Rotherham, Sheffield straight on, Gainsborough, Doncaster to the right, Newark, Lincoln if you go back.'

'Caw, it's just like filling in your Littlewood's being around here. Come on. Let's go to bloody Sheffield.'

It was getting faintly light in the east.

CHAPTER X

Alf, handcuffed to Stan, stood by the hedge. Stan was flashing his torch across the field.

'Come on, chum,' pleaded Alf, 'let's get out of this here rain. I won't scram.'

'Well, your pal has.'

'He ain't my pal. Right sort of bloody pal he is. All he done is lose me my job. This'll mean my cards for me.'

'You want to think of things like that before you start breaking the law. Blimey, what's this?'

The other three policemen debouched from the side turning and came to Stan. Two of them were supporting the third.

'Got away,' said the sergeant. 'Nicked our car and all. Give him a bashing into the bargain, too, for all that he's about four foot high. Right desperate bastard. I don't wonder he done a murder.'

'Done a murder, has he?' Alf's eyes were round. 'Coo.'

'Yus. Creased a tart.' Suddenly the sergeant realised what he was doing. 'Here, that's enough out of you.'

'Watchew going to do, Sarge?' asked Stan.

'You better go on the lorry with that client of yourn. We'll flag a private car. Better get into Newark.'

'Here, mister, don't go messing me about, I got to get up to Glasgow.'

'You got to do what you're told.'

'Here, Sarge. Here comes a private.'

Ponderously the sergeant stepped out into the road and waved his winking torch. The car swerved out of his way and carried on northwards.

'Thinks we're bandits now,' he said bitterly. 'Sauce, nicking our car. I'll give him knock-off police cars if I lay me hands on Mr Bloody Mathews.'

He spat on the ground.

'Here. You'll have to take us all back to Newark in the lorry.'

'Half a moment, mister, half a moment. There's a caff just a bit up the road. How about if we went up there, all had a nice cup of tea to keep us warm after being in the rain and you got on the blower and called up for a car.'

The sergeant looked at Alf for a moment. It was, he knew, bad for discipline, but still . . .

'All right,' he said. 'That's not a bad idea.'

'Here. What about taking this off of me.' Alf shook his manacled wrist. 'Can't drive like this you know.'

They unlocked him. Alf rubbed his hands together to get them warm.

''Nother thing,' he said. 'You can't all come in the cab, you know. There's only room for two. Three if one sits on the engine. Somebody'll have to sit on the load.'

'All right, Stan, you better do that. Come on now. We better get going.'

Alf drove them to the café. Reg's eyes glittered when Alf walked in with four policemen.

'Hallo, Alf,' he said. 'What *you* bin doing? Getting your-self into trouble?'

'Not arf. I should bleedin' say so.'

'Has a man with a muddy, dishevelled appearance, five foot four in height, wearing no overcoat, been in here?'

'Yes, mister. Left about twenty minutes ago with a tart.'

'With a tart? The saucy bastard.'

'Which way'd he go?'

'Ah, that *I* can't say.'

'Got a telephone?'

'Yes, mister. Round the back of the counter here.'

'All right. I want to use it. Give us five cups of tea.'

'Right, mister.'

The sergeant went behind the counter and telephoned. Alf drank his tea and began to worry Stan. He felt that he knew him better than any other of the cops.

'Hi, mister, how 'bout letting me go now? I give you a ride here, all said and done.'

'You better arst the sergeant.'

'He'll chew my knackers off.'

'Can't help that,' Stan's voice was coldly official.

The sergeant came from behind the counter.

'They're sending out a tender to pick us up and I got them to put out a call warning all the local forces.'

He picked up his tea cup and frowned. His station and the Yard had both been most uncomplimentary. Alf butted in.

'Can I go now, mister?'

'No.'

'Watchew want me for? You can't pinch me. I ain't done nothing.'

'You heard.' The sergeant was in no mood to be trifled with.

'I got my rights same as anybody else. Like that other bloke said you got to take me in custody.'

Reg was having the evening of his life. Such goings on.

'I will and all for obstructing a police officer if you don't watch out. I want a statement off of you.'

'All right. All right. I'll give it you. I'll give it you now. Only let me get on with me job and stop frigging about.'

'Right.' The sergeant took out his notebook and pencil. He was in no mood for dropping into any more trouble. Maybe this man's firm might kick up a fuss. 'What's your name? What firm do you work for?'

Alf told him.

'Got your heavy-vehicle licence?'

Alf showed it to him.

'Explain how you came to be in the company of the man Mathews and why you lied to me and the other officers.'

'Honest, guv'nor, I never knew his name was Mathews. Been all the same if I had of done. I didn't know you was after him. He come up to me at that caff and give me the fanny that he wanted a ride, so I let him have one. No harm in that. Lonely work driving alone at night . . . Up in that other caff, you know, outside Stamford, the bloke says as how the police was checking up on drivers and I got scared. I thought you was checking up on road girls or something and in case you told my firm I told this bloke to say he was working for the firm and all. I never knew you wanted him for murder. That's all.'

'H'm. I see. Where you heading for?'

'Glasgow.'

'Your firm got a branch there?'

'Yes.'

'I'll keep in touch with you there. We'll want you to give evidence when we get this man.'

'Don't get in touch with my firm, guv'nor. Whatever you do, don't do that. It'll mean my cards for me and that's a racing certainty.'

'You should have thought of that. All right, you can go now.'

'Thank you, guv'nor. You're a toff.'

Alf went.

CHAPTER XI

Shorty awoke with a start. He rubbed his eyes and wondered for a minute where he was, taking in the contents of the room. The cheap iron bed, the yellow furniture, the rug of plaited straw, the blue window blind that hung askew, the cheap pottery of the washstand.

Blimey, yes. He was in that Commercial Hotel in Sheffield.

Yes. That's all right, but where was Molly? Oh. There was a note on the mantelpiece underneath the engraving of 'Their First Quarrel'.

He got out of bed and stepped over to get it. The tail of his shirt flapped against his naked legs. His bare feet felt cold on the linoleum. He picked up the sheet of paper and read the message, which was written by a blunt pencil in misshapen letters.

'Woke,' it said telegraphically, 'and went out. Back soon.'

He lit a cigarette and, coughing a little, sat on the hard wooden chair.

What was the time? He would have to get out of here soon if he wanted to be safe.

He let his mind run over the drive in. They had come through Mexborough and Rotherham. At Rotherham it had been practically daylight. Trams were running and people were clip-clopping to work with heavy steps and wan white faces. Hooters had been proclaiming their melancholy signal that another working day had begun. Gaunt factory chimneys were smoking and great furnaces were helping to light up the pallid, half-hearted northern dawn. They had ditched the car in a side street. The various squeaks must have been in and a police car was certainly a little too hot.

A tram ride had taken them into Sheffield, where Shorty had taken a wash at a public lavatory while Molly booked a room at a cheap hotel. She had come out, fetched him, and they had gone back together. Once between the frowsy sheets they had both turned over and slept.

Sleep, bloody nice thing. Made you forget yourself a bit.

Shorty got up. The chair was damned hard anyway. He pitched his cigarette into the grate whose emptiness was decorated by a white paper fan. It smouldered there.

Where the hell had that dopey bitch Molly got to?

A heavy sense of impending doom hung over him as he walked across to the washstand. As he rinsed his face he felt the stiff bristles on his cheeks and chin. He had not had a shave since the afternoon before he had been discharged from prison.

When had that been? A hell of a time ago. Blimey, if only he had lost another day's remission. Caw, fancy Shorty Mathews wanting to spend an extra day in stir.

He dried his hands and face and put on his trousers. While he was fastening his braces the door opened. He ducked under the bed. Who was this?

Molly.

He got up again with an apologetically shame-faced smile.

'You can't be too careful, Kid,' he said.

Molly did not answer. She stood with her back to the door. He noticed that she had a morning paper under her arm.

'Good gel,' he said. 'Thinking of getting a reader. I'd like to know what's on. Anything in it about me?'

She nodded. He picked up his collar and tie.

'Aim it over and let's have a dekko. What's a time?'

'Half-three.'

'Blimey. Certainly had a good kip.' He turned away from the mirror. He had tied his tie. He noticed, for the first time, the dumb, beaten expression on Molly's face. 'What's a matter? Here. Let's have a look at that bloody paper.'

Panic seized him.

'You bastard,' she said slowly. 'You bloody bastard. You bin and murdered Alice.'

'Don't go shouting it all over the place.' He was beside her. 'Want everybody to hear?'

'You don't deny it then?' He had seized her wrist. She shook herself free. 'Hands off. You ain't going to do the same to me.'

He sat heavily on the bed.

'Molly,' he said. 'You got to listen to me. I never done it, see. She was dead when I got there. I lost me bleedin' head, that's all. Just lost me bleedin' head. How'd you expect a bloke with a record like mine to get away with it?'

'Lying bastard.'

'Don't you go calling me a liar!' Indignation made him bounce off the bed again.

'You dirty son of a bitch,' she said. 'You ought to be ashamed of your bleeding self. As if the girls didn't have it bad enough without poncefied bastards like you coming and murdering them. Me and all. I ought to be ashamed of helping you.'

'Listen, for Christ's sake, I didn't do it.' Shorty banged his forehead in impotent despair. If Molly wouldn't believe him, he had but a slim chance with the bogeys. 'She'd bin done in when I went there.'

'Watchew want to go running away for then?'

Molly twiddled her handbag in her fingers. She was not particularly interested in what Shorty might say.

'I lost me head. Besides, what chance I got, what bleeding chance I got? Blimey, even you don't adam and eve it.'

Molly sat down. She put the paper on the bed.

'Here, read this if you want to. It says all about you, believed to have headed north. Gives your description and all.'

He took the paper, glanced at it, then turned on her suspiciously.

'Watchew bin doing when you were out? You bin and shopped me. That's what you done. Come the copper. You dirty little bitch.'

'I never.'

'You did and all. Christ, you dirty little bitch. I got a good mind to smack you right on the kisser.'

'Want to murder another girl, do you? Just for that I won't bleeding help you, so there. I'm a prostitute admitted, but I ain't a copper. I come back to help you, spite of watchew done, and all you do is lie to me and call me a grass.'

'I ain't a liar.'

They sat on the bed, glaring at each other. Molly's curls bobbed beneath her hat.

'Watchew going to do?' she asked.

'Think I'm daft or something, do you? I ain't going to tell a little copper like you. I got me liberty to study.'

'Your liberty. Lot of good it done you. First day you're out of the nick you go and murder Alice. Pore Alice. Innocent as a babe unborn. Never did nobody no harm.'

Shorty made a gesture of despair. It was essential, somehow, that he convince Molly.

'How many times I got to tell you I never done it.'

'Take your dirty hands off of me. Murderer's hands.'

'Bloody hell, if you won't talk sense, I'm off.'

He got up and put on his coat and waistcoat. Before he could pick up his bowler hat she stopped him.

'Here,' she said. 'No, you don't. You don't go off without paying for this room. Think I'm made of bloody money, do you?'

He stood there, twiddling his hat in his hands.

'How much was it?'

'Half.'

He gave her the crumpled ten-shilling note that he had stolen.

'Cop. And now goodbye. I hope you die of pox.'

'I hope they top you.'

He picked up the golf clubs, then put them down again. There was nowhere that he knew of in Sheffield where he could sell them and he would look a fool carrying them around.

Out in the street he paused to think, rattling the few silver coins in his trousers pockets. It was a rain-washed afternoon. Busy people passed him. It would soon be dark. The sooner the better. He shambled off. There was nowhere in particular that he wanted to make for. Later he would buy an evening paper to see if there was any news.

He wandered through the uneven streets, gazing in shop windows, looking at the flapping, wet bills on the hoardings advertising shows at the local cinemas, glancing incuriously at the great gaps where houses had been pulled down in slum-clearance schemes. His shoes were worn through now. Once or twice he hawked and spat in the gutter.

For a time he stood in Fitzalan Square, watching the trams and buses. His mind was dull and he could not force it to think so he hung around, an inconspicuous and dejected figure. There are a lot of men like that hanging around in industrial towns. One of them spoke to him.

'Out of work, chum?'

Shorty nodded, but did not speak.

'Me and all. I can't get started nowhere. All this prosperity's joost paper talk, that's what it is, bloody paper talk. Bosses don't study us working chaps. Aye, chum. Joost so long as they're all right that's all they worry about.'

If Shorty had not been so depressed he would have laughed. To his Londoner's ears the Sheffield accent was irresistibly comic. The man shook his head and walked off. Miserable sort of a bloke, bowler hat and all.

Shorty's thoughts began to come more clearly. That there was nothing for him in Sheffield he knew. He had to get out. But where? How? He dare not go on the Great North Road. Anyway they probably thought either he was headed north or else making for a port. He'd go somewhere else. South, west, or somewhere.

Where the hell was Sheffield anyway? If only he could get hold of a map he might be able to weigh things up a bit. Public library, that's what he wanted. There was bound to be a public library. Better ask somebody. Better not ask a newsboy. They probably read their own bloody papers.

Blimey, one of the bills was:

MATHEWS MAN-HUNT: SOUGHT IN YORKS

Christ, Dick Turpin rode to York and all. Didn't do him no good, neither. They topped the poor bastard at Tyburn.

'Excuse me, mister,' he touched a man on the arm. 'Where's a public library?'

The man paused. His voice, when he spoke, was full of northern deliberation and well-fed rotundity.

'Up there, lad,' he pointed. 'Bear for t' left and then right. You'll find it. It's a new white building. Champion building. All come out of the rates.'

Shorty moved off on his wet feet. A hooter was announcing that work was at an end. Darkness was coming.

CHAPTER XII

A man was sitting in a cheap multiple tea-shop near Clapham Junction. He had drunk his coffee and was now nervously pulling a matchbox to pieces with nicotine-stained fingers. His lips slavered as he talked to himself. On the glass-topped table in front of him lay crumpled copies of the three London evening papers.

Two young clerks were laughing at the next table. The waitress came up to them.

'Pot of tea for two and one egg on chips twice, Miss.'

The waitress came, with tray on high, past the man's table. She had had a hard day and he could smell the sweat from her body. He thought with a laugh that if he put out his hand he could touch the pad of checks that dangled from her waist.

His eyes glittered. Then he remembered what the smell reminded him of. He put his hand in front of his eyes for a second to drive out the memory. When he looked up he could see the two clerks whispering to each other. They laughed.

Startled, he jumped to his feet, pulling his shabby mackintosh together over his food-spotted suit.

They were laughing at him. He knew it, he knew it.

He went up to the desk to pay his check. Standing there, waiting for the girl to press the button that would send his change tumbling down, he glanced back over his shoulder. No, neither of them was looking at him.

He sighed and went out into the street. For a while he stood, with his eyes pressed against the windows of a big store, watching assistants putting underwear on a figure.

One of them noticed him and nudged the other. He moved off. Near the station there was, he knew, a shop that sold copies of cheap American sex magazines.

A knot of girls got off a bus at the corner, so he stood watching them. His pupils dilated as he stared at the seams that ran up the back of their stockings.

He clutched hard the coins in his pocket, trying to make out, without looking, which were copper, which were silver. Yes, he had enough.

He crossed the road to take a bus up to the West End.

Before he arrived at the Latchmere, he got frightened and left the bus, the conductor looking curiously at a man who had only used a pennyworth of a fivepenny fare.

He walked back to Clapham Junction, talking to himself. Although he was only an out-of-work schoolmaster, financed by the charity of his relatives, he was cleverer than Scotland Yard. They were on the wrong scent.

He would take a little walk, just a little walk, to see whether anything interesting might happen, he decided, and then go home to bed. It was just as well to go to bed early. If anything went wrong he did not want the landlady to say that he had irregular habits. No!

He stopped and pulled at his nose.

If he stayed out a lot she would get mixed about what nights he had been out and what nights he had been at home. One had to be clever. Everybody was against one, everybody was trying to set traps. It was a great pity that it was so long before the end of the month.

He chuckled.

Well, just as soon as it *was*, and he got his cheque he would have a nice night out and a nice excuse, too. The difficulty was that so few of the girls liked to have one stay all night.

He walked on a little and then paused to look in a shoe-shop window. There was nothing much to look at here. Of course one could hardly expect a shop in the suburbs to be up to the standards of that one in Wardour Street.

He found his footsteps carrying him towards the station and the little stationer's shop.

After all, why not? One was going to be good tonight. Not going up to the West End. If he was to have an early night, he might as well choose something nice to read. It was going to be so lonely sitting there by the oil stove with the gas bubbling in the incandescent mantle. He was going to be scared, too, waiting up during the night and wondering if the footsteps coming down the street . . .

His throat went dry, and he shivered, standing at the street corner. A policeman, strutting on his beat, eyed him curiously. So he moved on quickly. As he walked he built up a fantasy world.

He was so clever that he had outwitted Scotland Yard. Of all the people in London they never guessed that it might be him. The perfect murder. Murder was a nasty word, but still, the perfect murder. Novelists were always writing about it, but he had done it. How many of the idiots walking around realized that he was a dangerous criminal, a prince of crooks? He would like to tell them and see their silly faces, these horrible, smug, lower-middle class people whom he had always despised and always envied because they had niches in the world, jobs, homes, people who were fond of them, instead of relatives who contemptuously tossed one a monthly pittance. He would tell them he was the Killer, no, the Lone Wolf. Yes, that was better, the Lone Wolf.

As he walked along he curved his fingers and drew back his lips in a snarl. Nobody noticed.

Look. They were cringing already. They feared him. The power of his eye. Women trembled and recoiled, repelled, but fascinated. Once they were in the clutches of the Lone Wolf it was too late. They were lost. Look. Even that beef-fed bully, that blue-coated clown of a policeman feared him. He dared not touch him, though he knew the Lone Wolf, that Napoleon Of Crime, the undetectable, the mastermind, was passing him by, so closely, so closely.

Exhausted by his game he stopped outside the shop he had been seeking and turned over the magazines on the trays. He could not make up his mind which to choose.

He was an old hand and knew that they were all gyps. The magazines that professed to print true confessions of amatory experience were the worst of the lot. That one which had stories about flagellation was probably the best. At all events its correspondence and its extracts from the press were always worth reading.

With his selection under his arm he went into the shop and handed the girl the sticky coppers that made up the purchase price. He said nothing and he avoided her glance. He knew his cheeks and ears were red.

When he got outside he rolled up the magazine and put it in his pocket. He did not want everybody to see it as he strolled on. He resumed his fantasy.

Even that girl in the shop, strange customers though she must see, had been so terrified of him that she dared not meet his eyes. She knew him for what he was – the candle that singed the wings of the poor moths. Poor moths.

He shook his head sympathetically.

Riches, position, power. He had everything. A Rolls-Royce to ride in, baths scented with strange oriental perfumes, jewels, exotic orchids and strains of sad, sweet music that lifted the hearer on high into realms of impossible bliss, subtle drugs unknown to Western science, he had them all, all. And yet, like Harun ar Rashid, he condescended to walk here among the multitude, in the midst of the poor people of Battersea and Clapham, wondering if by chance he might not find something new to enchant his jaded senses.

A slow, weary smile played round his mouth.

'Look out where you're going, clumsy.'

A stout woman, with a perambulator that held not only a baby, but her shopping, was glaring at him.

Really, the most impossible people nowadays. Of course, what *could* one expect in a district like this. Still . . .

He raised his hat, bowed, and smiled.

'A thousand pardons, madam.'

She stared after him as he shambled away with his shabby raincoat flapping.

'Caw. Ah well, least said, soonest mended, that's what they say. Poor feller must of done his nut.'

He got on another number 19 bus and, for the second time, paid his fare up to the West End. On the upper deck of the bus, a man was sitting behind him smoking shag in his pipe. He did not move, although the smoke worried him and made him feel sick, because, right across the aisle from him, was a girl, whose red hair curled over her cheek. At the top of Sloane Street she left the bus and he made as if to follow her then checked himself.

Twice he had paid his fare right into the West End and he was determined not to let London Transport get away with it twice. The Napoleon Of Crime, the creator of insoluble murders was too clever to let them outwit him over a mere matter of bus fares. Besides, she was almost certain to have rebuffed him. She had not even looked round.

All the same, while the bus waited at Hyde Park Corner for the lights to change, his mind was full of her and of her only.

What had she got off there for? Top of Sloane Street? Knightsbridge was obviously foreign to her. She must have been going into the park. Into the park. If only he had gone up to her and suggested a walk in the park. That was cheap. It might have only meant the price of two chairs.

With his masterful way of treating women, he would

have tucked her arm in his and they would have strolled under the trees, while she looked up at him, listening to his bright cynical talk, with smiling eyes. Everybody would have taken them for a pair of lovers. Interest in him would have quickly ripened into love. Warmed by his charm, excited by his dextrous loving, she . . .

The lights changed and the bus started with a jerk. His thoughts had excited him so much that he finally did let London Transport win and alighted at the corner of Bolton Street. The girls up at this end of the town were, he knew, far too expensive for him, but still he liked them accosting him. That is *when* they did. Most of them weighed him up at a glance and knew he was no use. He passed them furiously with his chin thrust up into the air like an insulted dowager.

It was funny, he thought as he walked along, the way the districts changed. At one time you never saw any of the girls on Curzon Street and now there were always four or five.

He made his way through the modern substitute for Lansdowne Passage and up Hay Hill. At the corner of Bond Street he watched a man being stopped by a tall French girl. He was breathing so hard and his heart was beating so fast that he thought he was going to faint. When the girl put up her hand to stop a cruising taxi he felt quite dizzy. She got in, with her client, and showed a length of silk-clad leg.

With bitter anger he walked on. These French girls were good. They knew how to make things exciting, how to do things that the English ones either could not or would not. But he could not afford them. For him all there could be was a dirty drab in Lisle Street who would take his ten shillings. He sighed and crossed the street. The course on which he intended to steer was by Vigo Street, Glasshouse Street, Denman Street, Rupert Street. All along the route there would be girls.

At the corner of Regent Street he counted the coins in his pockets. Three pennies, a half-crown, a florin, four shillings, two sixpences. Nine and ninepence. Nine and ninepence?

Agitatedly he stood there turning the coins over, feeling their milled edges. Surely he had made a mistake. Surely one of the pennies was a half-crown. None of the girls would ever look at anything less than ten shillings. None of them.

He dared not bring his money out and examine it in the light. If he did he knew that his worst fears would be confirmed.

A dead calm fell on him. It was over. He was out of luck. He would have to go home. Perhaps it was just as well. It would have been silly to have spent all that money. Still, if he had not bought the magazine, if he had not wasted that unnecessary bus fare, even if he had not bought the three evening papers, which he could have seen quite well at the public library, he would have been all right. Ah well. It had to be.

He would just walk back to the Green Park and take a bus home. Of course, hidden in his room he had those two pound notes that remained out of his month's allowance.

Don't be silly, if one spent that, well, ten shillings out of that wouldn't be missed. Not just ten bob. A mere half-sovereign. But it was silly to go all the way back to Clapham Junction and come all the way back to the West End. Well, he could go to Brixton. Plenty of them in Brixton or Streatham.

Quite cheerfully he went back along Vigo Street. He had never had a girl in Brixton. New fields to conquer. The breaker of women's hearts was going to go to a new district. Some unsuspecting girl was there in Brixton now, hoping for a client, little knowing, never guessing whom she was going to have. The Master Mind, the Subtle Sex

Slayer who baffled Scotland Yard. The Subtle Sex Slayer who baffled Scotland Yard. God. That was a good phrase and it was true too. So true, so very true.

His eyes narrowed.

If he could baffle Scotland Yard he ought to be able to baffle one of these silly girls. That should be child's play.

Again his breath grew short, again his heart thumped. He would. Yes. By God he would. He'd let one of these girls pick him up and talk her out of the fee, but he would have to be very clever, very subtle.

He was in Bond Street again. A girl was passing him. She wore impossibly high heels and flounced her buttocks saucily. She gave him just one look and passed him. Anger seized him. The little bitch. Yes, her. He chose her. He'd make her pay for that insult, pay for it, pay for it.

With an effort he controlled himself and, turning round, walked back after her, throwing out his rigid legs at a strange angle. He soon caught up the slowly-strolling girl and passing her raised his hat, believing in the truth of the counsel to treat whores like ladies and ladies like whores. He felt that that was just part of his irresistible charm. She looked him up and down with a cool, appraising glance. The twitching of his face muscles was the only thing that betrayed how this infuriated him.

'Well?' she asked, stopping, but still waggling her buttocks.

'What are you doing?' he asked fatuously.

'Looking for somebody with some money.'

His eyes went bloodshot. This was what angered him so. No technique, no finesse. The first thing they mentioned was always money. They delighted in rubbing home the insult that only by purchase could one have half an hour of female society. Still, he must play his part.

'How much d'you want?'

'More than you've got, sweetheart. Two pounds.'

'Don't be silly. Two pounds,' he echoed it scornfully, although it was all the same if she had asked for ten. He had to be crafty. 'I'll give you thirty shillings.'

'Got thirty shillings, dear?' Her voice was faintly incredulous, but she did not want to drive a client away.

'Of course I've got thirty shillings. I've got more, but that's all you're going to get.'

'All right, darling,' she took his arm. 'I'll go with you for thirty bob. My flat's just round the corner.'

'Oh, let's take a taxi.'

It would be silly now to spoil the ship for a ha'porth of tar. The longer she thought he had money the better. He held up his arm to a passing taxi. They got in. She gave the driver the address.

'Live all on your own?' he asked.

'Of course,' she said. 'I've got a nice little flat. You'll like it.'

'Don't you live with another girl?'

'Don't be silly. That's all finished now. They're getting very hot now, dear, the coppers. If two girls share a place they always pinch the one whose name the lease is in and charge her with brothel-keeping. Here we are.'

He paid off the taxi while he opened the door.

'Don't be naughty, dear,' she said wearily when he pinched her bottom as she led the way upstairs.

She opened the door of her flat and they went in. He looked around carefully to see whether anyone else might be there. It seemed as if there were only one room with a door leading off it.

'What's behind that door.'

'Bathroom,' she said. 'Don't you want to wash first, dear? There's a good boy.'

'Yes.'

He opened the door. Sure enough it was the bathroom

all right. He washed his hands under the tap and came back. She was sitting on the bed half undressed.

'Nice little flat, isn't it?' she said. 'I'll give you my phone number so you'll be able to call me up any time.'

'Good.'

He took off his coat and started to undo his tie.

'Here,' she said. 'Come on, dear.'

'What d'you mean?'

She made a counting gesture.

'My little present, please.'

'Oh, yes. The thirty shillings I promised you. Of course, of course. Look, I'll make a bargain with you.'

'What is it?' she interrupted watching him suspiciously.

'You be extra specially nice to me and I'll give you two pounds.'

'Let's see it first,' she said.

'Oh no, no. I'll give it to you after, if you're specially nice to me.'

'Don't talk soft. Gimme it now. I don't believe you've got thirty bob, or two pounds neither, come to that. All you're after is a cheap sensation. You want to see a woman without any clothes on. Well, you're out of luck, see. You're not going to waste my time. Bloody sauce. Come on. Get out of it.'

'My good woman, you can't talk to me like that.'

'Who can't?'

'You can't.'

''Ark at him.' She gave a raucous laugh. 'Who'd you think you are, the Dook o' Wapping?'

'You'd be surprised if you knew,' he said. His anger had mounted to full pitch and his eyes were blazing. He took a step nearer.

'Go on,' she laughed. 'I can hardly bear to wait. Tell me. There's a sport.'

He was right up close to the bed. His pale face was glistening with drops of sweat.

'I'm a murderer,' he said slowly.

'Go on! So'm I! Shake!' She held out a hand. 'Come on, unconscious, get out of it. I got the rent to earn.'

'I'm the man who killed that girl Alice in Drummond Street.' He ignored her words.

'Don't be silly. It's that bloke Mathews what the police are after. I read a bit in the papers about it. Seen his pictures in the papers and all. He don't look a bit like you. You can't kid me.'

'The police are wrong.' His words were slow. Fire had left his body and he was ice cold. 'I murdered her. Just like I'm going to murder you.'

'Gawd!'

Her scream was strangled into a snarl as his fingers closed about her windpipe.

CHAPTER XIII

Shorty came out of the public library.

Nottingham, he said to himself. Nottingham or Derby. Derby'd be best. It's on the main drag from here and a bloke could make his way along to Liverpool later when it had got a bit quieter. Still, Nottingham would not be so bad. The frog and toad led straight from there to Cardiff. The first thing was to find a transport caff.

He wandered back to Fitzalan Square, with the instinct that always makes bums head for the centre of any town. He had seen the local evening paper in the library and what he had seen had neither cheered him up nor dispirited him any further. The police of Lincolnshire and the West Riding of Yorkshire were searching for him. They said that they had a clue, but then they always said that. You could gamble on it as a racing certainty. There was nothing to worry about in the police having a clue. That was what they were for. Just to have clues, the big mugs.

He stood around in the square for a while looking about him, making up his mind whom to ask. There was a man waiting at the tram stop who looked like one of the Irish tramp navvies. Shorty went up to him.

'Excuse me, china,' he said. 'I'm on the road. Can you tell me if there's any place in this town where a bloke can pick up some transport?'

The navvy scratched his head.

'Well now,' he said, 'there's Glossop's the haulage contractor. They're a Sheffield firm. You might be getting a lift from them and you might not. Sure, I'd say you might not. The drivers would be scared to give you a ride and this the town they're working in. It's a hell of a town, so it is, to be stranded in, Sheffield.'

'You're cheerful, all right,' said Shorty. 'You don't think I could get a lift anywhere around here?'

'I do not. You're in Yorkshire now.'

'Ar.'

'Them Yorkies never was any good. Ah, they wouldn't give a blind man a light. Are you holding any cash?'

'Un-unh. Not much, but I have a bit.'

'I tell you what I'd be doing, son, if it was that I was like you are. I'm working now, thanks be to God, but I have been on the road in me time. Scotland, Kinlochleven and all them places, Wales, Cardiff, Swansea, every county in England bar none, I've been in them all, working on public works and travelling as best I could from one place to another job. Do you want to get out of Sheffield, now?'

'Yes, for Christ's sake. I told you that. Aren't there any caffs here where the transport drivers pull in?'

The navvy scratched his chin.

'Well now, cafés now. Ah, there might be, so there might. Let me see now, never worry, I'll tell you what to do. You'll do best to go to a café. Do you know Wicker Bar? You do not. Well, there's some cafés there.'

'Where the hell is Wicker Bar?'

'Go down there to your right and follow on across the river, the River Don they call it, God knows why, and cross over the river until you see a viaduct across the road. There's plenty of cafés there, but God knows if you will get a ride. Ah, here's me tram. I can't stay here chatting all night. I must be getting back to me lodge to have me tea.'

'Okay. So long.'

Shorty walked off downhill into an industrial quarter. He found plenty of cafés and, going into one, sat down at a table. A waitress came up and resting her hand on the table shouted angrily: 'Well?'

'Large tea, two rashers, two fried eggs and a piece of fried bread.'

It was just as well that he had still some of that silver left. He was feeling hungrier than hell. He hadn't eaten since . . . since a hell of a long time anyway.

A bloke at a nearby table was wearing a driver's blue-peaked cap. Shorty leant across to him.

'Got a wagon outside, mate?'

'Aye.'

The driver went on eating. He tucked a piece of bacon into his mouth with the blunt edge of his knife.

'Where going?'

'Chesterfield.'

He was wiping his plate with a piece of bread. The waitress brought Shorty his order. He set about it. Well, the eggs were certainly good. Chesterfield? Where was that, for Christ's sake? Oh yes. On the road to Derby. The driver had pushed his plate away and was smoking a cigarette.

'Give us a lift there?'

'Aye.'

He sharpened a match-stalk and picked his teeth. Shorty went on eating. Nobody could say these Yorkies had much to say for their bloody selves. He took a mouthful of tea. This little tightener was sure going down well. It was just what it took. He finished his meal and lit a cigarette. The driver got up.

Blimey, thought Shorty, I left all that bleeding whisky back in the hotel. That was a shame if ever there was one. Ah well. Too late to worry about that now.

'Ah'm going now, chum, if you want that ride.'

Shorty followed the driver up to the counter. They both paid their bills and then went out and got into an almost brand new Morris truck.

'What you got on board?' asked Shorty as they drove off through the drab streets.

'Noothing mooch. Only empties.'

Well, if a bloke didn't want to talk he didn't want to talk and that was all there was to it. You couldn't argue about that. Anyway this was a hell of a lot more comfortable a cab to ride in than that cold bastard he'd had last night. Poor old Alf. Well, he certainly copped out.

'New bloody trook this,' said the driver suddenly. 'Gaffer's gone daft or summat.'

'Yes?'

'Aye. Nuthing would suit him but he had to change all trooks. Good thirteen months life i'them and all. Reckon he's got more money than bloody sense, that's what Ah reckon. Change bloody trucks when you relicense boogers that's what Ah say. Some sense i'that. Ah was happy wi' old trook and now he gies me this new hoor.'

'Yes?'

'Aye.'

Just as suddenly as he had become conversational he dropped off into silence. The lorry had been badly loaded with its empties and as they rattled about the weight got still more unevenly distributed. He had a hell of a job keeping the wagon straight on the camber of the road. It was quite dark now and cars passed them with a swish and a momentary glare of their headlights.

'What town's this we're pulling into?' asked Shorty at last.

'Chesterfield. Where'd you want to be set down?'

'Any place'll do. I'd like to get some more transport on to Derby.'

'Ah.' The driver sucked his teeth. 'Bloody oonlikely to get that, chum. You ought to have copped a leap back there in Sheffield. Reet oot o'luck. Ah tell you what. Two mile out of town there's a caff. Tha might pick up some stuff there as will take you through to Derby. There's stuff that goes Sheffield, Chesterfield, Derby, Burton,

Birmingham. This do, if Ah set thee down here, reet by Crooked Spire?'

'Sure, one place is as good as another. Thanks for the ride.'

Shorty walked on. He saw a signpost directing to Derby and Nottingham. Handy things signposts. Saved a bloke from asking his way and so walking straight into a tumble. The Derby-Nottingham road must split just outside the town. Maybe it would not be such a bad bet if he went to Nottingham instead. Who knows but that bleeding Yorky didn't rumble him and put him away.

These short hops in local stuff were the best even if you didn't get such a long ride. Maybe by keeping to back roads and only taking local wagons to give him lifts he might finally manage to keep under cover until they had forgotten about him.

Forgotten about him? Blimey, that was a laugh. Slops were like elephants. Just like bloody elephants, clumsy, big-footed and all. And they never forgot.

He was walking now down a street of working-class dwellings. Lights shone in most of the windows and the flickering firelight played on the blinds. It was evening and most of the men were home from work. Even if they did have to work hard, even if some of the poor bastards were out of work, even if their homes were uncomfortable, over-crowded, cold and drab, at least they did have homes. They had somewhere to keep out of the rain, they had someone who was interested enough in them to bawl them out.

He walked on and on and on. The steely rain was wetting him through. His ill-fitting raincoat made him clammy and sweaty. The next house he screwed he would have to look out for a nice little pair of shoes. These bastards he'd got on wouldn't see him much farther if they lasted out at all. He was walking on his uppers now and having even worn a hole through his sock, winced every time that his wet sole came in contact with the pavement.

Two miles out of town the Yorky had said. Hell of a long two miles. The houses were thinning out and there were rank patches of grass and weeds interspersed among the allotments and the tin cans. A young man with a girl on his arm, coming from the other direction, passed him. First envy, then tolerance.

Good luck to you, kid, you'll need it. Blimey, a girl never brought a bloke any luck. If it hadn't of been for Alice he wouldn't be in this jam. And that Molly. Caw, strike a light! Carrying on and rorting like that. Making it all the worst for you, that's what she bin doing. As if she didn't feel just as bad about Alice. Poor bloody Alice, well she had taken a bit of rough and all, when you came to weigh it up you was all a hell of a sight better off out of it. Even if they did nail him and top him so bloody what? It was that three weeks' waiting that got you down. And all that paper talk about the way they treated a bloke waiting execution. You wanted to be a cleaner in the Ville to learn just how true that was.

Kicked around from pillar to post, that's what he'd been all his life. Even when he'd been a kid up in Kilburn and hung around the caffs in the Edgware Road . . .

He walked on and on and on. The café never seemed to get any nearer.

CHAPTER XIV

A young man in a black Homburg and a teddy-bear coat came swaggering up Piccadilly and turned up Bond Street. He wore handmade brown brogues and had a little black moustache. He quickened his pace a fraction, not enough to be obvious, when he saw two burly men in raincoats and bowlers.

Of course, it had to rain tonight. The rent was due on both places, one of the girls had been fined the usual forty shillings that morning, and then it must go and rain just so as to spoil business utterly. Well, Pauline didn't seem to be around. She must have got a client.

He looked down Burlington Gardens.

No, she wasn't there.

With his hog-skin gloves he smoothed his moustache. If she had had anything like a decent night he would let her go. After all she was a good girl and a hard worker. Standing around on a night like this was a good way of getting ill. He couldn't afford to have either of his girls off the game just now. Besides if you were good to them, they were good to you. Never held out on you, or had any mess or any of that caper.

A girl detached herself from a group near the telephone booths and sauntered down towards him. She flashed him first a professional smile and then changed it to one of recognition.

'Hallo, Harry,' she said.

'Why, hallo, Queenie. How's every little thing?'

'On the ribs, dear. Right on the ribs.'

'Seen Pauline?'

'Let's think. Why, yes. I saw her; why it must have been three hours ago. She was getting into a cab with a steamer. Now I come to think of it, I haven't seen her since. She hasn't been round here as I know of. About half an hour ago I had a client.'

'Three hours ago, blimey. Client must have fell in love with her.'

They both laughed.

'Now I come to think of it, he was a funny-looking bimbo,' said Queenie. 'You wouldn't think he had any dough.'

'Well, sometimes it's the funny-looking bimbos that's got all the dough.'

'Ah well,' Queenie sighed. 'S'pose I'd better be getting back on the job. I got me rent to earn. Don't want Mr Johnson to catch me miking. Cheery-bye.'

'So long, Sugar. Save some of your love for me.'

Harry stood there. Three hours was certainly a long time. Still she might have had another client. Perhaps he'd better just slip round and see what was on. Wouldn't do any harm. Anyway he needn't actually go into the place. After all Queenie had said the steamer was a funny-looking bimbo. Nothing like taking care of your girls.

He strolled round to the flat and let himself into the front door. Wide move that to get a spare set of keys cut. Agents always looked a bit funny about it, but you never knew when they were going to come in handy. Much better to do it on your own. He listened outside the door.

It didn't sound as if there was anyone in there. He turned the handle and walked in. Three minutes later he was outside in the street. His face was as white as his silk shirt.

Now he *had* got to box clever. Let's see. Alibi. Yerce. That was okay. He'd been playing billiards round at the Club with the boys. Not that their word counted for much. Still. The bogeys were bound to pin it on him. They'd been after him for hours and years. Best thing was to go straight to the station and see them. Take the wind right out of their sails. Have a drink first, they'd be bound to hold him for hours questioning. No, if he had a wet they were stone ginger to smell it and swear blind he was drunk and that he'd killed her in a fight. Besides, time. Bloody seconds counted in a job like this. You certainly had to use your loaf.

He walked into the police station.

'Yes, sir?' asked the officer on duty.

'May I see somebody from the Department, please?'

That mug calling him 'sir'.

'What d'you want to see somebody from the Department for?'

'I think there's been a murder.'

'A murder?' The officer raised his eyebrows. 'Just a minute, please.'

He came back with a plain-clothes man.

'The officer tells me you say you think there's been a murder, sir,' he began. 'Why, hallo, Harry!' His voice changed. 'Watchew want? Come on in here.'

He led the way into an office in which three other detectives were sitting, working and writing-up their reports.

'Here, boys,' he said, 'here's a stroke to come out with. Big Harry the ponce's come in and he's only said he reckons there's been a murder. Who done it, Harry boy? You?'

The other detectives got up and grouped themselves round.

'It's Pauline,' said Harry.

'You mean the girl you been poncing on?'

'I never ponced on nobody,' said Harry.

'All right, skip that for a minute. Let's get this

straight. What's up, Pauline bin and done in one of your other gels?'

'No somebody's done her in.'

The detectives looked at each other soberly.

'That's torn it,' said one of them. ''Nother of these bleeding West End murders. More trouble.'

'Who done it, Harry?' asked another. 'You?'

'I'll call the Yard,' said a third, 'and get them to send round a murder bag.' He grabbed a telephone.

'Sit down, Harry, and tell us why you done it.'

Harry sat down. He made an imploring gesture.

'Listen,' he said, 'I knew you'd say that. That's why I came straight round here. I never done it. I know you got it in for me, but I never done it. As God's my judge, I never. Soon as I found out I come straight round here so as to give you a chance to nick the bastard.'

He sat there with his black hat in his hands looking as ineffective and frightened as an English diplomat.

'Where is the body?'

'Round at her gaff.'

'Why did you go round there? You were there all the time, I s'pose.'

'No, straight I wasn't. I asked one of the girls where Pauline was and she's said that she hasn't seen her for three hours, so I went round just to see if she was all right.'

'How did you get in?'

'I got the keys.'

'So you've free access to the place at any time?'

'Yes.'

'Do you live there?'

'No. I live in Maida Vale.'

'What d'you want the keys for then?'

'Well, you know. Just in case I got to go round there any time.'

Harry was sweating, this was even worse than he had

feared it was likely to be. The detectives had formed a semi-circle round him.

'Look here, Harry boy.' The detectives changed their tactics. 'You're in a jam. You'd better come clean.'

'There ain't nothing to come clean about. I told you all I know.'

The door opened. Even this slight relief was heaven to Harry. He looked round gratefully. A uniformed constable, without a helmet, stood in the doorway.

'Yard car's here, Sergeant, with the murder bag.'

'Okay. We'll be going. Just run the rule over him, Ted.'

Only one detective was left with Harry. He pulled a chair up and started talking confidentially.

'Look here, son,' he said, 'there's been a lot of these girls getting creased. There's been a regular outcry about it. You'd better help us all you know or we'll mix it for you. You're in a jam, but we'll help you out. You *was* poncing on this girl wasn't you?'

'Well, yerce, I suppose I was if you like to put it that way.'

'Ever have any barneys with her?'

'No.'

'Sure?'

'Certain.'

'Well, you're a bloody miracle, straight you are and I ain't a-kidding to you. I never heard of a bloke and a tart, specially when they're in that racket, not getting rorting at each other. You got another girl and all, ain't you?'

'No.'

'Come on, tell the truth.'

This was only a bow at a venture but the arrow hit the mark.

'Well, yerce, now I come to think of it I have. Listen, mister,' Harry suddenly realized what he was saying, 'but you can't get me on that. She won't give evidence against me.'

'Uh-uh? Well, we'll skip that for a minute. Neither of these girls ever get jealous? Tell the truth now. You might as well save time.'

'Well, you might say perhaps they did.'

'You had a quarrel with this Pauline tonight over the other girl and done her in. That's the strength of it, ain't it?'

'I hadn't seen Pauline since yesterday.'

'Well, the other girl done her in?'

'No, blimey, no. She never.'

'How'd you know that? You were on the premises and saw who it was?'

'No. I was round at the Club, playing billiards.'

'Oh yeah? And I suppose there's a bunch of right spivs who'll give you as neat a little alibi as ever you see. Well, we got this far. You've been living on the immoral earnings of two women who were jealous of each other and one of them has been found murdered. You found the body, because you had the keys to the place? H'm. A very pretty story, a very pretty story.'

The door opened again and another detective came in.

'Watchew on?' he asked.

'Cow got creased,' Ted said. 'Just running the rule over Mr Johnson.'

'Interesting.' He hitched up his trousers and sat down on the edge of the table.

In the meanwhile the man in the shabby raincoat was walking rapidly westwards along the Victoria Embankment. Every time that a tram passed him with a roar, a rattle, and a glare of lights he started out of his skin.

The Lone Wolf. Boy, would Scotland Yard be baffled. Lone Wolf strikes again.

He touched his pocket. Inside were three pound notes that he had taken from the girl's handbag. Three pound notes. He would be able to treat himself to something nice. Was the Lone Wolf clever in eluding the police dragnet? Ha! Ha!

At the corner of Piccadilly he had taken a number 9 bus and had ridden eastwards into the deserted City. Frightened of his own footfalls in the echoing caverns of the deserted streets he had come back, glancing cautiously at the tall City policemen, through Queen Victoria Street and on to the Embankment.

The Master Mind had thrown off the pursuit. There was no-one on his trail. Like the cunning fox – no, that was a mixed metaphor, one could not be a Lone Wolf and a Cunning Fox. Still he had doubled back on his tracks. Nothing was so easy as fooling these fools. A keen brain, strong nerves. That was all it needed. Who had a keen brain? Who had strong nerves? Who, but the Lone Wolf?

The tall buildings of Scotland Yard on his right frightened him, so he went down the steps on to Westminster Pier and stood for a little while watching a string of barges making their melancholy way upstream. Big Ben struck the quarter-hour. He glanced up at the illuminated face and, seeing the light burning above, realized that Parliament was still in session.

The High Court of Parliament now assembled. Tomorrow they would be asking questions about the Lone Wolf. The Honourable Member for somewhere or another would ask the Home Secretary if he had any information about the assassin in their midst, the terror that walked by night.

A police car gonged its way out of the gateway of Scotland Yard and roared down the Embankment. He looked apprehensively over his shoulder until it was out of sight.

Ha! So the chase was on! Police cars scouring London. Little did they think that their quarry was almost within their grasp had they but the brains to put out their hands.

A river-police launch chugged its way downstream.

Even on the water the vast organization was searching for him. An Ishmael. Every man's hand against him. His hand against every man. And every woman.

A policeman, on beat, on the Embankment above his head, shone his lamp down.

'Hallo, what you up to? Thinking of committing suicide?'

'N-no, officer, no.'

'Haven't you got no home to go to? Standing around in the rain like that. Catch your death, that's what you'll do. Why don't you go down to the Night Office down by Charing Cross Bridge. They'll fix you up with a kip if you're stuck for one.'

'I'm all right, officer. Really I am. I was only looking at the river. I wasn't doing any harm, really, officer.'

'You want your brains tested, that's what you want,' the policeman grumbled, moving off with the rain glistening on his cape.

Ha. That was a close shave for the Lone Wolf.

He walked rapidly through the subway and came up in Westminster.

It would be silly to go home now with this money in his pocket. The silliest thing in the world. The really clever thing to do was to double right back on his tracks and go up into the West End again. Nobody would think of looking for him there. Nobody. Nobody. Besides, with all this money on him. Anyway on a wet night it was less noticeable for one to be out in the West End.

He started off up Whitehall.

Suddenly he put his hand to his mouth.

He would have to go home some time that night or his landlady might suspect. Last time he had stayed out all night with the other girl. The other girl. This one had been nicer. It had been more fun. Lots of girls. Lots and lots of girls. Trembling. Gasping.

CHAPTER XV

Molly sat in the back of the car with Eddie's arm round her waist. Ron was driving. It was a tough break for him, he felt. Molly felt someone was seeing to it that she was getting tough breaks, too. As if it hadn't been bad enough to have got herself tied up with that swine Shorty – and God knew how much he had dropped her in it – she just could not make out in Sheffield. Nobody didn't seem interested. She had even gone into three places that looked as if they might be all right and all it had meant was expense. It didn't half run away with a girl's money if she just kept on having to pay for herself. There was no fun in that.

At one time a policeman had spoken out of turn to her. Reckoned he was going to nail her or something for soliciting. Sauce she called it, proper sauce. Didn't half give her a turn. Last time had been way up in Lancashire and she certainly had a job with them. If it hadn't of been that she used her loaf they would have tried to send her to a home and reform her. Go to a home. Not likely. Far better to plead guilty, sauce the Lady Missionary and do seven days instead of paying the two nicker. Reform! Caw. They didn't half think up some strokes.

Good job she'd got out of Sheffield. Hot town, proper hot town. No sense in doing seven days if you didn't have to. Blimey, no.

She didn't fancy these two clients she was riding with. Funny, she never fancied going for a ride with two at once. Some of these stories you heard nowadays made your hair curl. Never knew what they were going to get up to next and that was a fact.

Gutter-crawling they'd been and all. You got a funny class of fellow gutter-crawling now. It wasn't what it used to be. Engineers they said they were. Like as not the car was knocked off.

'No,' she stiffened and pushed his hand away.

'Don't you love me any more?'

'Go on. You are a one. What next, I'd like to know.'

Ron turned his head round jealously. The bloke at the back always got all the fun.

'What you up to, Eddie?'

'Just showing the little lady my personality, that's all.'

'Your personality. That's a good one. Never heard it called that before.'

He swerved over to the left to avoid an oncoming car. The buzzing of windscreen wiper was beginning to get on his nerves. It was hell driving in the rain.

Eddie held Molly to him tightly. He rubbed his cheek up against hers. His face was bristly and his breath smelt.

'Where you taking me to?' asked Molly.

'Heaven, sweetness, heaven.'

'Don't talk silly. You are a funny boy. Regular cough-drop, that's what I call you. You know perfectly well what I mean.'

'Where are we heading for, Ron?'

'Oh, let's have a drink in Chesterfield. Say, did you ever hear that joke about the fellow who went into a tobacconist and said: "Packet of Chesters, please."'

Eddie groaned.

'For God's sake, Ron. I've been hearing yarns from you all the bloody week.'

'Your language,' said Molly mechanically. It was just as well to let a fellow think you was a refined type of girl. Respected you for it they did.

'P'raps the girlfriend hasn't.' Ron was determined that

Eddie wasn't going to get away with everything. Acting the big shot that way. After all whose car was it?

'Tell it to her sometime when you're alone together.'

'Who says we're going to be alone together?' said Molly.

Eddie laughed and rubbed his cheek against hers again.

'Do you know something, darling, you're the kind of girl I like. Got a comeback, that's what you've got. Let's go to that place at Tupton, Ron.'

'No, nuts, let's stop in Chesterfield, we're practically there now. It's lousy driving in this rain.'

'Don't be silly. It's only about five miles on to Tupton and you can park on the road there. You can't do any parking in Chesterfield.'

'I suppose you're right,' grudged Ron.

'You see, I think of everything,' said Eddie.

'One of the clever ones.'

'Yes, darling, one of the clever ones.'

'You're so sharp, it's a wonder you don't cut yourself. Go on. Stop it now. We're driving through a town. Whatever'll people think.'

'They'll think what a lucky guy I am sitting in the back beside you.'

'Don't you tell the tale?'

'Don't worry, my love, we'll be out of town soon and it won't matter what the people think and I'll show you I can do something beside tell the tale.'

'You don't hate yourself, do you?'

'Not nearly so much as I love you.'

'One of you love birds pipe down for a minute and light me a cigarette. I daren't take my hands off the wheel. This road's as slippery as hell.'

Ron had to do something. Eddie was having far too good a time. Even getting a cigarette off them bust things up momentarily. He was damned if he let Eddie get away with it. Spin a coin. That was fairest. Spin a coin to see who was going to be first.

Smoking the cigarette he drove carefully through Chesterfield. He couldn't afford another blister and they were bound to say there was a girl in the car. The firm got damned annoyed if you took a car out in your spare time even though you paid for the petrol.

Chesterfield and its crooked spire were behind them. Eddie started showing off again.

'Let's park here, Ron.'

'Use your nut, man. What, right on a main road? I'll drive slowly and see if there isn't a farm road we can back up. There's bound to be police cars around looking for that chap Mathews or whatever he's called and they're likely to turn nasty. I don't want to get mixed up in anything. Yes. This looks okay. Hold tight, I'll back up a bit.'

He backed the car about ten feet up a farm road and switched off the headlights. He turned round to the back seat. His heart was beating faster and faster.

'Just a minute. Don't be so rough. Can't you behave?'

Molly was having a tough time with Eddie. He was determined to forestall Ron. After all he had been chatting her all along. She was his girl by rights.

'Stop it, Eddie. Do try to show a little decency.'

Eddie sat up indignantly.

'What's a matter with you, old man? What d'you think we brought the girl out for?'

'All right, but let's play the game by each other. How about flipping a coin up?'

'Okay. Have it your own way.'

Ron put one hand over half a crown that he had balanced on the back of the other. He was feeling magnanimous now. After all it was an even money bet.

'Go ahead, old man,' he said. 'Call.'

'Head.'

'It's the lady. I win. Go and take a walk.'

'What, in the rain?'

'Hey, don't I have a say in the matter?' interposed Molly.

'Well, damn it, I won the toss, didn't I?'

'Yes, that's fair enough. He won the toss all right. Go on, kid. Show your sporting instincts.'

'Yerce, but aren't you forgetting something, you boys?'

'What?'

'Aren't you going to give me a little present first?'

'Aw nuts, sister, you don't expect that, do you?'

Molly wriggled herself free from Eddie's arm. This was more than a joke. She wasn't going to wear that sort of a caper.

'All right, then nothing doing.'

'Come on, be sensible,' Eddie slid his arm round her again. 'I thought you were a nice girl.'

'I thought you was a decent feller and all. Taking a girl out and treating her this way. You ought to be ashamed of yourself, you ought.'

'It's an awful long way home, kid, and a nasty wet night.'

Ron had crawled over the seat by now and was sitting in the back. Molly's heart sank. She knew her chances were pretty bad now. Leaning over she fumbled for the door handle and let down the window by mistake.

'Oy, shut it up. Letting that draught in.'

'Where's the handle? I want to get out.'

'What d'you want to do that for?'

'Well, if you won't come across, I won't neither, so there.'

Bluff, she felt, was the only card to play.

'That's what you think, sister.' Ron caught hold of her. 'You're going to kick through whether you like it or not. You'd better face up to that.'

It was stone ginger that they weren't going to drop her no money now. She could bet on that. At first dull acquiescence and then rage came over her. Why the hell should they, the bastards? She tried to push Ron's arm away.

'I'll scream the place down,' she threatened.

'Scream away, my darling. Nobody'll hear you.'

She lunged out with her feet and caught Ron a welt on the shin. He yelped, let go of her and grasped his leg. She caught hold of the handle and got the door half open.

'You little bitch. You'll pay for this.'

Ron caught hold of her coat. She turned round and bit him in the wrist and he let go again. Eddie made a grab at her just as she was getting her legs out. She slipped and fell, screaming, half in, half out of the car. Ron, his temper thoroughly up, grabbed her round the waist and tried to pull her back. Her hat fell off. She kicked and screamed and struggled.

'Come on, Eddie, give us a hand for Christ's sake.'

Eddie opened the door on his side, hopped out, ran round the car and tried to push her in. She lashed out with her legs and caught him in the stomach. He sat down in the mud with a surprised look on his face.

'Help, help,' she yelled. 'Bloody cowards. Call yourself men? Two of you and one defenceless girl. Help! Help! Help! Murder! Rape!'

Ron tried to put his hand round her mouth. She bit his palm, but all the same he did not let go. His blood was up and he was all out to get the little bitch. Eddie got up. God damn it, fancy a girl making a fool of them like this. He tried to catch her flailing feet. One of them struck him on the nose and sparks danced in front of his eyes. He made another pass and succeeded in gripping one of her ankles. He tugged and pulled. Surprisingly to him, his task was easy. She came out of the car with a rush and falling on top of him rolled in the mud. Ron came tumbling out after her, but managed to regain his foothold. Molly struggled to her feet and kicked Eddie in the face before she tried to run, but she had lost a shoe and Ron was on her. He tried to pick her up, but she kneed him in the stomach. He staggered and steadied himself with a hand on the bonnet. Eddie got to his feet again. He was smothered in mud, and blood was streaming down his face. Molly, who had never ceased her ear-piercing screams, tried to dodge past Ron.

A funny short figure paused at the end of the lane and then came running down towards them shouting: 'What's up? What you on? Your holidays or something?'

'Help! Rape!'

The newcomer leapt at Ron and banged him in the face with a left-hander, at the same time bringing up his knee. This was too much for Ron. He just couldn't take it twice in one evening. He grabbed for the bonnet of the car, but his nerveless fingers slithered off and, doubling up, he fell into the mud. Molly's rescuer rushed at Eddie, swinging lefts and rights at his head. None of them connected, but they made Eddie retreat.

'Stand up and fight, you dirty yellow bastard. Come on. Have a go.'

At last a swing landed neatly on Eddie's ear. He was off his balance and staggered. His assailant was on him and let him have it.

He grabbed the sheik by the back of his neck and rained short right-handers into his face remorselessly. Bang, bang, bang, bang, bang. It was an eternity of pain for Eddie. His mouth was lacerated, his nose crushed, he dared not open his aching eyes. Suddenly his body went limp and his attacker let him fall to the ground and lie there with his gurgling breath bubbling through the blood.

'Well, lady? That's just about finished them off. Pity they didn't know how to fight or we might of had a nice little bundle.'

He rubbed his bruised knuckles and then peered forward through the rain.

'Blimey, Molly.'

'Caw, Shorty.'

'Stone me.'

'Well?'

They laughed awkwardly and then Molly shyly kissed him. Grinning he slid a triumphant arm round her waist.

'You certainly sorted them out.'

'Yerce. I didn't do so bad.'

Ron stirred and struggled into a kneeling position, agony making him clutch himself. Shorty moved to stand over him threateningly with his right arm drawn back.

'Want a bit more?'

'No.' The word was an almost inaudible gasp.

'Well, on your way then, feller, if you know what's good for you.'

With one hand on his middle and the other on the running board he managed to get on his feet.

'This – is – my – car.' Each slow word was a torment to his pain-racked body.

Shorty looked at Molly.

'What we going to do? Leave them to look after their bleeding selves and nick the car?'

'Use your loaf, mate. We put ourselves in wrong then. We got an open and shut bloody case against them.'

Ron staggered forward a step and sat down in the mud.

'I got a good mind to finish you off, you yellow cowson,' said Shorty.

Trying to cross his hands to cover his frightened, pain-wrecked body finished Ron off. His trunk sagged against the car. Shorty looked at him contemptuously, then spat in his face.

'How's the college friend getting on?'

He walked down towards Eddie, who lay on his back,

weltering in the mud, trying to summon up enough energy and courage to get up. Shorty tucked a toe under his body and then turned him over on to his face. The bold would-be rapist offered no resistance, so Shorty came back to Molly who, having just recovered her shoe, was standing on one leg to put it on.

'Come into the office, kid,' he said. 'Stroll down the lane a bit. I want to go into conference.'

With linked arms they walked down the lane. When they were out of earshot of the others Shorty spoke.

'Listen,' he said. 'We got to think up something. What did Mussolini and Hitler get up to?'

'Well, they was gutter-crawling, see, and they picks me up. When it comes to the time, they've said they ain't going to give me me drop, so I turned round and said no dice and after a bit of argy bargy they sets about me and then you've turned up.'

Shorty stroked the back of his puzzled neck.

'We got to box clever. If you try to nick them all they got to say is that you're a common prostitute and that I committed an assault on them. Your word and mine don't count for damn all. Oxo, that's what they're worth. And I can't give evidence, neither. Not the way things are with me.'

'Ar.'

'How about just nicking their car and leaving them to walk home.'

''Tain't worth it.'

'Well, how about this, then? I put the fear of Christ into them now. They don't know whether they're on their arse or their elbow. I'll get them to drive us down the road a piece, down to Derby or one of them places. They'll do any bloody thing I say. Then I'll say when we've hit the town that I'm putting in the squeak. They'll come across with all the dough they got to be out of that and we'll be laughing. What you say?'

'Sounds all right, but make it Nottingham, that's on a lorry route. Derby ain't. Besides it's a lousy pox-hole anyway. I want to get to Coventry.'

'Okay. Come on, let's go.'

They strolled back again, Shorty rubbing his knuckles as they walked.

'Me old German Bands ain't half sore.'

Eddie and Ron were both on their feet. Shorty went up to them.

'Listen,' he said, 'you bastards are driving us down to Nottingham.'

'I'm not sure I can drive. I want a doctor.' Ron was still gripping himself.

'Have it your own way. I'll drive the car into the nearest town and send a copper out to nick you then. Unless you'd like the clipper again instead.'

Ron cringed away. Shorty lifted his hand to him.

'Get in the car, you,' he commanded. 'Get in front. I'll drive. Where's the starting handle?' Groaning, Ron handed it to him. 'Here, Molly, cop this. If Gentleman Jim starts anything, let him have it.'

CHAPTER XVI

Outside the café the wind whistled its way across the York-shire moors. Inside Alf and Bill sat by the smelly oil stove and talked.

''Nother cup o' tea, mate?' asked Alf.

'Yeah. Don't mind.'

Bill got up to go to the counter, but Alf put out a restraining hand and made him sit down.

'I'll get them.'

'Keep your lob in your pocket, Alf boy. You'll need it.'

He went up and came back with two cups of tea. Alf stirred his cup moodily, the spoon rattling.

'Here,' he said, 'what kind of a reference d'you think I'll get?'

'That I *don't* know. He didn't half seem bloody angry when he called me into the office and told me to come up here and take over your wagon.'

'Seemed bloody angry and all over the blower. 'Tain't my fault. I ain't done nothing wrong. Good driver I am, never been in no trouble. Well, not to speak of, and then to get this here.'

He took out his pay envelope and from the buff cover drew out the folded sheet of notepaper to read it for the hundredth time. On it was typewritten: 'The Aberdonian Transit Company Limited regret that they have no further use for your services. Enclosed is the sum of six pounds, six shillings and fourpence, being wages for two weeks less insurance, ten shillings bonus for trip and one pound for travelling expenses. On your return to London you will call at the office in order to collect your insurance cards which have been stamped up to date.'

'Making me give you a receipt and all. Lousy bastards. Think all their drivers are crooks or something.'

'You'll be able to get another job all right. You've still got your heavy-transport licence. It's when you lose that it's a bastard.'

'There's plenty of good drivers walking around unemployed with heavy-transport licences in their pockets and all.'

'Get a job in London, driving a laundry van or something.'

'Yes? Working all day and half the bloody night and be under the guv'nor's eyes all the time. I'd like to break that bloody Mathews' neck. Dropping me in for it like this, just when I was getting set nice and all. I'll never do nobody a good turn again, not in my bleeding life.'

He lit a cigarette violently, and threw the match on to the floor.

'What kind of a bloke was he? This Mathews, I mean.'

Alf rubbed his chin with the back of his hand.

'Oh, I dunno. Ordinary sort of a little bloke. Somewhere round about twenty-six I reckon. Didn't have much to say for himself. You wouldn't put him down as a bloke what had just come out of the nick and done his tart in.'

'Didn't he look a murderer at all?'

'No. Well, not my idea of one.'

'I suppose he did do it?'

'Police reckon so all right.'

'Them bastards!' Bill spat contemptuously on the floor and then ground his heel on the gob. 'A bloke with your experience of transport driving ought to of got more sense than believe bloody coppers.'

'You're right and all. Swear your life away for three ha'pence.'

'How'd you know it ain't the same with this poor cowson? Just come out and all. They probably got it in for him the way they do. Still, it'll all come out later, and anyway he'll get a fair trial.'

It was Alf's turn to be contemptuous.

'Fair trial? Yes. Same as the firm give me. I don't get a chance to say nothing in my defence. Out I go whether I like it or not just because I done a bloke a good turn.'

'One thing I don't follow,' said Bill, trying to change the subject away from Alf's misfortunes of which he had already heard enough, 'is where he gets hold of this pusher they've got a bit about in the papers.'

'Told you that. He's picked her up in that caff, see. The one I've bowled into with the coppers.'

'Yes, but there ain't hardly any girls on the road nowadays. Not this road anyway. Things ain't what they were. Used to be a bit of life about before when there was girls about and before this Act come in messing you about.'

'Yerce. Things were all right, then. Blimey, the times I've had.'

'Caw, hark at the old-timer.'

'Well, I bin driving since 1934. Great North Road all the time.'

'Great North never was much cop. Coventry Road, that was the one. Blimey, I remember when I was driving for the LMS . . .'

'You never worked for a railway.'

'I did and all. I worked for the LMS two years before I come on this firm.'

'You ought to be ashamed of yourself.' There was genuine horror in Alf's voice at the thought of his mate having worked for a railway company. His rising, indignant tone awakened another driver who was sleeping with his head pillowed on his arms.

'What's up?' he asked.

'My mate's just said he worked for LMS before he come on the firm.'

'What's wrong with that?' The awakened sleeper shared but little interest or indignation.

'Yerce,' joined in Bill, 'that's all over and done with now. Railway's same as anybody else. Just as good mucking-in chums as any of the drivers.'

The other man sat upright. He was older than either of the two Aberdonian Transit drivers and, judging from the badge he wore in his peaked cap, he drove a Leyland.

'It's all different now,' he agreed. 'I been driving since 1923 and when I first come on the road, blokes working for railways dursn't come into a caff unless they was four- or five-handed. The other boys would've soon given them what for if they'd tried any of that caper. That's all done away with now. There's no fun left on the road. Nothing but hard graft.'

He felt in his pocket for his cigarettes, but went on talking.

'You know what started it all? You see, when road transport first started there was none of these big firms. Most firms didn't have no more than four or five lorries and the guv'nor or his son was usually a driver and all. Any road, he was a working chap same as the others. Then the railway companies suddenly turned round and said: "Blimey, why should the transport blokes come cutting into our trade like this?" so they bloody well start having lorries of their own and all. Well, it ain't fair their big organization against the little blokes, so that's where all the troubles started.'

'Ar,' said Alf, nodding his head.

'But it's all big firms nowadays,' the Leyland driver continued. 'Bout's, Fairclough's, London Scottish, Aberdonian Transit, Glossop's, Fisher Renwick's, they're all just the same as the railways.'

'But there's plenty of independents left. Blokes working on their own and all,' said Bill. 'Bags of them.'

'Yerce, but every year there's less and bloody less. No, the road isn't what it was. When I first started driving, a bloke never knew how far he'd go in a day. He just bloody well drove on till his bloody eyes was falling out of his head and then he had a kip in his wagon. You dursn't do that nowadays. I've heard of drivers getting blistered for that. "Having a mechanically-propelled vehicle not under proper control." That's what they get you for.'

He paused to hold a match to his cigarette that was bobbing, unlighted, between his lips.

'Bloody fortunes that've been made out of the road and all. I know blokes that started as drivers and ended up managing directors.'

He blew out a cloud of smoke. 'And the tarts, now. Take the road girls. Prostitutes, that's all they are now, what's left of them. When I first started there was lots of girls who went on the road just for the fun of it. Decent brought up girls, servants, factory tarts and all that. Not the riff-raff you find now. You'd see them at a weekend sitting in bloody droves along the fences and all you had to do was take your choice. They'd take a ride south on a Saturday night, say, and then go north on the Sunday, and be back at work on Monday morning just as if nothing had happened.'

He paused, then added as an afterthought: 'Didn't want no money for it, neither. Most of them.'

'Caw,' said Bill. 'Bin nothing like it in my time.'

'Course there ain't.' He nipped his cigarette and put it behind his ear. 'You youngsters don't know what driving is. I've drove practically everything in my time, steamers, fourgons, all that caper. Plenty of work, plenty of money and plenty of fun. That's what it was like in the old days.'

He chuckled.

'Blimey, the things I've seen in some of the caffs, particularly on the Cardiff Road. Make your hair curl and I ain't a-kidding to you neither. Fights and girls and Gawd knows what. I've known blokes playing nap with a tart for the kitty and she sitting on the table strip-naked. I was sitting in on that game and all, but I didn't make out. No, it was a bloke driving a furniture van that copped that time. It was the girls spoiled the bloody road in the end. Them and the big companies. When these old cows started to come for rides things got different and with copping a packet, well you got to do something about it. But them days I'm talking about all the girls was out for was just a lark and if you wore a lorry driver's hat you was a little tin god and in some of those caffs on the Great West you used to see blokes and tarts in evening dress and furs and all that madam eating bacon sandwiches along with the boys.'

'Well, I seen that meself and all,' said Bill who was just about as browned-off with the old-timer's reminiscences as he was with Alf's bellyache. 'Ain't nothing in that.'

''Tain't the same as what it used to be. Can't be. Stands to bleeding reason it ain't. There's a different spirit about today. That's what, there's a different spirit. Which firm do you work for?'

Alf and Bill exchanged a grimace.

'Aberdonian,' said Bill. 'Well, that is . . .'

'He does and I used to. Got the sack. He's been sent up north to take me wagon over.'

'Got the gooner? That ain't no good to you. What with all this paper talk about prosperity and rearmament it's harder than ever it was to get a bloody job, that's what it is, harder than bloody ever. I don't know what they mean talking about a boom. They must have done their nuts or some bloody thing. What'd they give you the bullet for, chum?'

'Cowsons.' Alf eagerly leapt into a fresh recital. Bill

tried to be big-hearted and not sigh. 'I give a bloke a lift. Well, how'm I to know who he is? Seems all right, ordinary sort of a bloke. Well, it's turned out he's only Mathews, that geezer they're looking for for the Drummond Street murder. That's all. The sweenies stop me and this Mathews gets away and then they get me firm on the blower and I'm out of a job. Give me a week's wages in loo. You must of read about it all. It's been all over the papers. A bloke in Doncaster give me half a quid for me photo. I don't know what it's going to come out like.'

Alf smirked with conscious pride.

'Blimey, so you're the bloke. Watchew going to do now?'

'Christ knows. Go back to the Smoke I reckon. I got to get me cards. They sent me money up here by Bill – he come by train.'

'One thing about Mathews,' said the Leyland driver. 'He's got plenty of bleeding nerve. Nicking the coppers' car. You got to admire him for that. I like anybody who puts them cowsons in the crap. Bastards.'

He spat on the floor.

'That's right.'

'Bastards.'

'Your mate going on up north with your wagon?'

'Yerce.'

'How you getting back to the Smoke?'

'Train, I reckon. Me firm sent me a quid for the fare.'

'A oncer? That won't bloody well take you from York-shire to London. Besides, you'll want all the rent you've got while you're signing on. Train. Blimey. Call yourself a driver. Whyn't you get a lift from somebody going south?'

'Werl. That's an idea.'

'Of course it's an idea. You want your nut seen to. You get yourself into it by giving a bloke a lift and you haven't the eighteenpence to ask for one yourself. Caw. I don't know what drivers are coming to nowadays. I'll give you a ride if you like. I'm going down to the Smoke.'

'Okay, mate. That'll save me a bit of dough. But I don't want you to lose your job and all, same as what I've done.'

'I don't bleeding want to lose me job neither. I'm a married man meself with three children and I got their pictures in me pocket here to prove it if you don't believe what I'm saying, but I'll always help another bloke that's a driver and chance it. Live and let live. That's my motto.'

'Thanks, mate. You're a toff.'

'I ain't. Just another driver, that's all. Come on. Let's have a cup of tea and a bacon sandwich all round and then we'll get started.' He raised his voice and yelled at the counterman: 'Three teas, three bacon sandwiches.'

CHAPTER XVII

Shorty drove carefully. It was the best thing to do. Without a licence and with every flat-footed son of a bitch in the North Midlands looking out for him the less risks he took the better. Tupton, Clay Cross, Higham, Alfreton all slipped underneath the wheels of the car. Nobody had spoken for three-quarters of an hour. Every now and then he had glanced up at his driving mirror to see if everything was all right with Molly. The windscreen wiper buzzed like a swarm of bees. The slanting rain glittered in the cones of whiteness from their headlamps.

'You want to bear left through Ripley if you're going to Nottingham.'

Ron's voice broke through the silence and darkness. Its sound even frightened him. Shorty jerked his head round to the left with the snarl of a scared animal.

'Shut up, you. Wait till you're spoken to.'

'I was only telling you.'

Ron's tone was aggrieved. He was gradually recovering his self-confidence, although he ached with pain and drying mud.

'Can't help that. I want less of your old gup. Pipe down.'

'Listen, you can't kidnap us like this.' For a long time Eddie had been trying to pluck up the courage to speak. From the very first second that he had heard the sound of his own voice he grew more and more at ease. 'This is robbery with violence. Knocking us about the way you did and then pinching the car.'

'All right, all right. You want to get pinched for indecent assault, do you? Nice little charge that.'

'Two wrongs don't make a right.' Eddie was thrilling to the restoration of his courage. 'Besides, what the hell were you doing there? Knowing the girl, too. Something a bit funny about that, if you ask me.'

'Nobody's arsting you. Give him one over the nut with that little persuader.'

'No. Let baby have his talk, it'll do him good.'

Ron joined in again. Once more Eddie was taking the lead from him and he was not going to stand for that.

'Yes,' he said. 'This is *my* car, you know. What d'you propose doing when you get to Nottingham?'

'That's my business. You'll find out.'

'It's going to look very funny if you try to bring a court case. This is Ripley . . .'

'Believe it or not,' said Molly.

'Go on. Bear left and then sharp left again about five miles down the road. You want to go through Eastwood and Kimberley. Yes it's going to look very funny if you try to bring a court case. What were you doing there? Why didn't you take us to the local police? That's a couple of questions you'll have to answer.'

Shorty drove on. He did not take any notice of Ron's questions. Eddie chimed in again.

'If you don't do anything about this, I won't either. So there. Let's call it a deal.'

Again Shorty made no answer. He was trying the difficult job of driving on a dark, wet night along a road he did not know, without having to lower himself by asking Ron to repeat his instructions.

Ron tried again. After all, they would be in Nottingham pretty soon. He had not the remotest idea of what was in this fellow's mind or what effect he was having on him, so he changed his tactics.

'Look here, old man,' he said, 'you're a man of the world, you know how things are. I mean to say, after all, haven't you ever picked up a girl and taken her for a ride in a car? I mean – damn it. I know p'raps we did go a bit far, but after all I don't see why you, you know what I mean, a court case and all that, because although we'd get away with it and all that sort of thing, you know what I mean, it's going to make things pretty awkward. Between you and I, we'd probably lose our jobs.'

'Yes,' said Eddie. 'You don't want to go and ruin our lives just for an evening's entertainment.'

'You bastards,' said Shorty coldly, not taking his hands off the wheel or his eyes off the road. 'Just for that I got a bloody good mind to put the squeak in about you. I had meant to let you go, I don't mind saying, but now I'm going to hand you yellow rats over to the cops. You can't fight, you bellyache and moan when you think you're getting into a jam, and you call half killing a girl an evening's entertainment. I'll bleeding well fix you. You cowsons.'

'Here,' said Molly, scared. 'You can't do that.'

'Who says I can't? You ain't turning yellow and all, are you? You'd like to see these sons of bitches nicked?'

'Course I would. But, gorblimey O'Reilly, you know why you can't.'

'All right, all right. Don't shout about it. I got a good mind to go through with it come what bloody may.'

'Use your loaf.'

'Here, what *is* this?' Eddie turned round in the back seat and stared at Molly. She could see his pulped white face shining in the darkness. 'Why can't he go to the police?'

'Give him one, Molly.'

'I'm going to get to the bottom of this.'

'Oh, you are, are you?' Shorty stopped the car and switched off the engine. 'You're going to get another good hiding if you don't watch out.' He kicked Ron on the shins. 'Where are we?'

Ron gripped his leg and then let go with a groan.

'Between Eastwood and Kimberley,' he gasped. 'Get me a doctor, for Christ's sake.'

'Yes, I know, but where the bleeding hell's that? How far off Nottingham?'

'Nine or ten miles. I'm going to die, I think. I can't stand this pain.'

'Bloody well murrer then. As for you,' Shorty had glanced up at the mirror. 'You leave that girl alone. If you lay a finger on her, I'm going to kick your pal just where it's going to hurt him most, and if he kicks off you're going to have his blood on your head. See? Now, listen, I'm starting this car again and I don't want a blind word out of either of you.'

He started the car and drove off. His mind was going round in circles. This needed a hell of a lot of thinking out. More bloody thinking out than he could manage anyway. Molly had got him rumbled all right. Just a matter of time before these bastards had got him weighed up. They'd go straight to the cops and put him away. Gamble on that. If he made them get out of the car now . . .

He was driving so badly now that he narrowly missed crashing head on into a lorry. He slowed down. A bloke couldn't think and drive.

They knew that he was going to Nottingham. Unless he pulled out of there and got across to Derby or some bloody place. Yerce. Oh, bloody hell. He had a good mind to drive the bloody jam-jar straight up a telegraph pole and finish the whole goddamned thing. Sick of being badgered and bitched about from place to bloody place. No sense in that.

Christ, if there were only some warm, comfortable bloody gaff he could get into and stay in, and sleep and sleep and sleep until it was all over and forgotten. Some fur-lined gaff. Allen, now. They'd topped him all right. He was bloody done for, but he didn't have all this bloody worry. Caw strike a light, the worst bloody part of it was all this chasing a-bleeding-bout and the headlamps of over-taking cars shining through the rear window and dazzling you.

'Here, got any dough?'

He nudged Ron.

'Yes, why?'

'Just wondering. How much you got?'

'About a couple of quid. That's got to last me till pay day.'

'How much has chummy got?'

'What d'you mean?'

'How much money does the old college friend have with him?' Shorty tried out a BBC accent.

'How much money have you got, Eddie?'

Eddie fumbled in his pockets.

'About twenty-three bob.'

'Couple of Lord Nuffields, ain't you, riding around in a car and all without the price of a drink in your pockets. Blimey, I don't know what things are coming to. Well, any-way, I'll make a deal. We don't want the police in this. Anyway you reckon you don't and it won't help neither of us to know you're in the nick. I'll be big-hearted. I'll drive you both on to Nottingham and get out of the car there and we'll say bygones are bygones if you each of you hands me over a oncer. How about that?'

'Well, this has got to last me till pay day.'

'Sorry mate, I can't help that.'

Ron realized the finality in Shorty's voice. He hastened to cover his mistake.

'Well, let's call it ten bob apiece.'

'A oncer a head or I'll have you nicked.'

'What d'you think, Eddie?'

'Aw nuts, this is blackmail.'

'Yes? You want to do about eighteen months for indecent assault? All right. Have it your own way. I don't mind. Only don't blame me when you're doing time. I give you your chance.'

'I think we ought to, Eddie.'

'It's all right for you, but it only leaves me three bob.'

'I mean if this comes out . . . Damn it all, you can pawn something.'

'Well, if you say so . . .'

'Come on, make up your minds. We're coming into some big town now and it looks mighty like Nottingham to me. You ain't got much time. You don't want me to stop next to that policeman over there and give him the office, do you?'

'Here,' said Ron hastily. 'Here's mine. My share.'

He dived into his pockets, groaned, and handed over a pound note.

'Okay, mate. You're out of it. This only leaves Mussolini to pester up if he wants to be in the clear and all.'

'Here you are.'

With an aching body Eddie leant forward and dropped a pound note over Shorty's shoulder so that he could take it with his left hand.

'Okay, mate. Well, this little job's over. The car's yours now. Always at your service, gents.'

He pulled the car into the kerb and got out.

'Come on, kid, we're off.'

Molly pushed open the door and got out too. Before the two of them moved off into the suburban darkness, she turned round and waved an ironic hand.

Eddie leant back against the upholstery and sighed.

'Well, we're out of that, thank God.'

'Fat lot of use you were.'

'Well, you didn't do so good yourself.'

There was a moment's silence. Then Ron spoke.

'Well, what're we going to do?'

'Go back to Sheffield and sleep it off. It's all a bad dream.'

'Yeah? Well, you can drive the car for I'm damned if I can.'

'Oh hell. Let's go and have a drink first. It'll do us good. Damn it we need it.'

'What are we going to use for money? You've only got three bob or so.'

'I've got an extra pound. I was holding out on that chap. That's why I was arguing with him to save time. I had a hand in my pocket all the while, trying to separate two notes, one from each other.'

'Good boy. I'm glad we beat him at something. Well, what's wrong with this pub here? I suppose we can leave the car.'

They got out of the car and made an agonizing way across the road to a public house. The three steps that led up to the saloon-bar door were torture. The barmaid looked curiously at their muddied, blood-stained figures.

'What's it going to be?' asked Ron, supporting himself with one hand on the bar counter.

'Brandy. Yes. Make it a brandy.'

Eddie sank into a high-backed chair and put his hand up to his face. He breathed with his mouth open, but all the same great waves of pain burned through his nose. He lit a cigarette and threw it down into the fender. It hurt his lacerated lips too much for him to smoke it.

Ron came over to him. He held two glasses of brandy and soda in between the fingers of his left hand, his right clutching the lower parts of his stomach.

'Here you are.'

'Thanks.'

Eddie took the glass, set it to his lips, then held it away. Even the diluted spirit burned like fire.

'My God.'

'What's up?'

'Your face. God, I feel ill. We've got to get to a doctor.'

'Yes.'

Another customer came into the bar and looked away again with raised eyebrows. Eddie picked up a copy of the *Nottingham Journal* that was lying, folded, over the wooden arm of his chair. He tried to hide his face. He held the paper up for half a minute.

'Good God!'

'What's the matter?' Ron leant forward. 'Oh, hell.' He groaned and pressed hard against his stomach.

'Look at this, man. Look at it for God's sake.' The excited words croaked out from between his battered teeth. 'Who'd you think that bloke was?'

'What bloke?'

'That bloke who came along. The one we – er – had a fight with.'

Pride made his mind seek euphemisms.

'Let's have a look.'

Ron stretched out a hand for the paper.

'Look. It was that bloke Mathews. The murderer they're combing the country for. Good God.'

'Quick. Let's see.'

Ron looked at the paper, with bent and concentrating eyebrows.

'You're right,' he said, then looked at the paper again. A moment later he looked up and caught Eddie's eyes.

'I'm going to the police about this. He can't get away with all this violence. That explains why he didn't want to say anything about us. It's all quite clear now.'

'Don't be silly. We'll let ourselves in for it.'

They were speaking in hurried whispers. Ron tried to make an impatient gesture. He frowned with pain.

'They won't worry about us. Not if we catch a murderer

for them. Besides, we've got to. It's our duty. It's not safe to have a man like that around.'

He got up and staggered towards the bar.

'Got a telephone here?'

'Yes.'

The barmaid put her hand up to her hair.

'Call the police. Ask them to send a car round at once.'

'Why, what's the matter? What's wrong? There's no need to have the police here. I'll have to ask the guv'nor first.'

'Can't you see I've been hurt? Hurry.'

'What's it all about?'

'I've been in touch with Mathews – Mathews, the Drummond Street murderer. They're searching the country for him.'

'Here, what's all this going on? Trying to start something?'

The portly figure of the guv'nor came behind the bar. He glanced first at the other customer, then at Ron and Eddie.

'Evening, Tom. What's all this? Coming in here in this state you two and kicking up this row. Don't serve them, Mabel.'

'I want her to call the police. My friend and I can tip them off to Mathews, the Drummond Street murderer.'

'Call the police office, Mabel. We'll get to the bottom of this. If you're telling lies I'll give you in charge.'

'I'm not telling lies.'

Ron sat down abruptly.

CHAPTER XVIII

The West End was gay with its last flicker of life before the streets were given over to the night birds. Sky signs tumbled and danced their chromatic electric dances, commission-aires called cabs, people with voices unnaturally loud took emphatically affectionate farewells, bums walked around with despair in their hearts, wide boys looked out for a chance to nick a wallet or buzz a moll.

Among the crowd, walking with bent, out-thrust head, was a man with his hands deep in his raincoat pockets. For a few minutes he stood on the edge of the pavement in Piccadilly Circus, a little frightened at the traffic. His walk had tired him and put his nerves on edge again. Up Whitehall he had come and then across the frighteningly wide expanse of Trafalgar Square. And then he was terrified.

The main streets were too wide, too well lit, so he had walked up Oxendon Street and then along Orange Street until he found himself in the Haymarket.

This was too bad, the way that he kept on running into danger. It would be far safer for him in that Fun Fair. He went and gambled a few pennies without having the luck to win even one packet of five cigarettes. Icy despair gripped him. He was out of luck.

'Change me sixpence, please.'

He touched one of the attendants on the arm and got his coppers.

Now the necessary score on that machine, he thought, is 7000. If one could get, say, 5000. No, that might be too difficult, 4500 with one try, everything would be all right.

He put his penny into the slider and started playing. The first ball scored him 600, the second 300 points. Nine hundred for two. Sickening fear clutched at him. The third ball bumped its way among the electric sparks. The machine clocked up another 400 points. God, please make the score come out right. The fourth ball brought his total up to 2100. In despair, he played the last one and scored 1000. Three thousand, one hundred.

Oh, never mind about the bet. Have another go. Get 4500 this time and everything would be simple.

He had gambled away his last copper coin before he was satisfied, but the sixth penny brought him a score of 5100. With a gay swagger of confident shoulders he walked through the Sports Garden, looking with bitter envy at the boys who were strolling around arm-in-arm with their girlfriends. In Coventry Street he paused to weigh the situation up.

A magnet was luring him to Bond Street.

After all, why not? The police were incompetent idiots. How could they be expected to catch a Master Mind like the Lone Wolf even if they dared lay their sacrilegious hands on him?

A thick-set man, wearing a black hat and an overcoat with widely-padded shoulders, dug a similarly-dressed acquaintance in the ribs.

'What ho, how you going on?'

'Mustn't grumble. Wages, just wages. Heard the latest?'

'No? What?'

He glanced at the Napoleon Of Crime, weighed him up as some old bum, nothing worth worrying about, but lowered his voice. His voice was, however, not quite as low as he had hoped.

'Someone's creased Pauline.'

'What, Bond Street Pauline? Blimey.'

'Yerce. And they've knocked Big Harry off.'

'They must of gone doolally. What they want to do that for?'

'Don't arst me. All I know he's at the station now. They're running the rule over him.'

'Caw. Nobody ain't safe, nowadays. Not the way things are.'

With a self-satisfied smirk the Napoleon Of Crime walked on. Ha! So they had arrested the wrong man again. The dolts! In his own rough, uneducated way the man had expressed the truth. 'Nobody ain't safe nowadays.' And nobody was. Criminal or prostitute, even policeman. None of them was safe when the mastermind wove his wicked web.

So he stood on the kerb, a little frightened at the traffic.

At last, with his quick jerky steps he went down the stairs and crossed by the subway. There was a sweet smell of fruit down there, fruit from the shuttered fruit stalls, and of hot air that swirled around up from the escalators, of newspapers that had been trodden on by muddy heels. There were no girls down there any longer. Just like that film – *No More Ladies*. Once it had been pleasant to saunter round the Underground circus and look at the bodies for sale. Now the goods were offered on the cold and rainy streets.

He walked up Regent Street and then turned left down Vigo Street. Bond Street beckoned him.

It was fantastically easy to fool the police. The poor idiots would probably have expected him to have travelled up Piccadilly.

One or two girls moved forward from their posts in Burlington Gardens and Cork Street, but, seeing what was coming, fell back again. It was no use trying to put the hammer on a man like that. Irresistibly he was impelled to walk past the flat where, what was her name, what had that young ruffian called her? Pauline. Pauline lived. No, she didn't. Pauline didn't live any more. She was dead. Dead. No longer would Pauline pester men and ask them for money. The Avenger had met her. Vengeance is mine.

He walked past the flat and noticed that a police car stood by the open door. A uniformed constable with his thumbs in his belt was on guard. He paused at the little patch of light that shone on the pavement. His watery legs would carry him no further.

'Come on,' the policeman's voice was gruff, 'on your way now. If you haven't got a home I can soon find you one.'

He swallowed and hastened past the door.

The impudence of the man, daring to speak in that way. Of course he did not know whom he was addressing. Once again the Avenger had eluded the ever-reaching, ever-failing arm of the law.

He ducked round the back way and found himself in Bond Street once again. At the corner, three girls were talking together in whispers. One of them raised her voice a little and he heard the end of what she was saying.

'. . . care what he says. I'm going on home. It's a lousy wet night anyway. There's not much chance of anything. Get your death of cold standing around even if you don't get murdered.'

Frightened, he skipped across to the other side of the street and walked rapidly, with swinging arms, in the direction of Piccadilly.

Even the very girls on the street were conscious now of his power, of the influence he had over them. They fell back before his glance, trembled and talked to their fellow wretches about going home. But grimly like, like an Avenging Angel, no, a Cleansing Flame, the mastermind strode through London's streets and nobody knew where he would strike next.

He turned east along Piccadilly, waiting for the traffic lights to change. A girl looked at him curiously and whispered to another as he passed. He hurried on, fragments of their conversation straying to his ears.

'. . . Pauline . . .'

'. . . talk silly . . . seeing things . . . whyn't you go home.'

His heart hammered in his throat as he hurried. Good heavens. Suppose that girl went to the police, denounced him. Oh, he could laugh it off. After all, what was the value of the word of a common prostitute? Well, he had to have an alibi for the night. He could say? He could say he had been to the pictures. What had he seen?

He picked at the quicks of his thumbs and ran his tongue over his crusted lower lip. Darting a quick look over his shoulder he slowed down his relieved steps. The girls weren't following him. They weren't even speaking to a policeman. They were just standing at the corner. Jauntily he strolled along.

Once more the Cleansing Flame had escaped the trap that had been laid for him.

His jauntiness degenerated into a limp. He had walked a lot that evening.

He was tired. He would cross Piccadilly and take a number 19 bus home.

Good heavens! It didn't matter about the alibi. It didn't matter even if he did not sleep at home that night. The relevant times were different. Well, he could stay out all night. He had money in his pocket. He could eat, he could drink, he could . . .

Home. It would be nice to lie in a warm bed, with folded arms against a snug chest, with the covers pulled well over the head, with the key turned in the lock. It was raining and he would be able to hear the raindrops spattering on the lead of the bathroom roof.

He started to cross the road, but the traffic was too thick. If he walked up to Piccadilly Circus he could cross by the island, he could even cross by the subway.

So the police had arrested Big Harry, had they? Who was Big Harry? He must be that wretched creature's bully. Despicable, loathsome. To think that a woman should sell her favours, insult a man by asking him for money, and then hand the money over to some oily brute. Good God, it was disgraceful.

A pang of joy ran through him at the thought of this Big Harry in the clutches of the police. Triumph. Revenge. So clever, but beaten at last. It would be funny if they hanged Big Harry. Very, very funny. At one blow the Avenger would have rid London of two germ centres. They called him the Napoleon Of Crime? He? The Lone Wolf? Nonsense, impossible. He was a public benefactor. His services were as useful to the community as, as, as a street scavenger's for example.

A little depressed at the comparison with a street scavenger he limped on.

It would be nice, very nice, very comforting, of course it was just an indulgence, but it would be nice all the same, to pass, just to walk casually past the police station where Big Harry was detained. Perhaps they were giving him the third degree, perhaps they were beating him up. The police were never very kind, one heard, to what did one call them? Ponces.

Unconsciously he was walking towards the police station. He halted at the foot of its steps and stared up at the blue lights.

So that was where Big Harry was.

He chucked his tongue.

Too bad, too bad.

He walked away, sorrowfully, with the stooped shoulders of an old and worried man.

It would be so nice in bed and he had got that copy of the sex magazine to read.

CHAPTER XIX

Shorty took Molly's arm and helped her. She was walking with a slight limp. She snuggled up to him a little.

'Blimey, kid, you very nearly dropped me in it. I shouldn't wonder if you hadn't made a tumble of it even now. You want to use your loaf. Bellering out like that like a bloody bull.'

'Watchew going to do now?'

Her grip on his forearm weakened. She felt a little timid of him.

'Get the hell out of this town. The bleeding heat's on here for me. I'll drop you one of them oncers and you can do what you bloody well please. You can't say I haven't played fair with you. I done you a good return for what you done for me.'

'You have and all.' She stopped talking and then impulsively caught hold of his arm more tightly than before. 'Oy,' she said, with beating heart. 'You don't want to get rid of me, do you?'

'It wasn't so very long ago you reckoned you didn't want to have no more to do with me.'

'Yerce. That was before you set about them geezers. Why'd you do it, Shorty?'

'Werl,' he was shy. 'Werl, it wouldn't do to have blokes setting about tarts that way.'

'What about Alice?'

'Never laid a finger on Alice. You know that. I told you.' His tone rose in a fierce crescendo. 'One thing more. Don't you think I come to the rescue because it was you. I didn't know who the hell it was. I'd of done the same for any tart, so there.' They walked on in silence for a little.

'If you want to stick around for a bit,' he said suddenly, 'you can. I don't mind. I ain't had a push in the truck since I come out of the nick and I'd like to have another before they top me. I don't see what good it's going to do you sticking around with me, I must say. Only get you into trouble, that's all.'

'Never mind about that,' said Molly irritably. 'Don't worry about me. I can look out for meself.'

'Bloody well have to. Now listen. We daren't stay here in Nottingham in case them two geezers rumble us and put us away. I'm going up to a bloke and ask the way to the station. It's a bit of a comedown to go by train, after riding around the country on a lorry like the bleedin' Dook O' Wapping, but they'll never think of us taking a cross-country journey on a rattler. I'll ask a bloke where the station is and you walk on ahead a bit first. If anything comes out about us two together it'll be a dead tumble if we've arst the way to the station.'

Molly disengaged herself and walked on. Shorty went up to a man.

'Where's a station, china?'

'Eh?' The man, like all Northerners, seemed unwilling to impart information. 'Which station d'you want? LMS or Victoria?'

'Victoria.'

Shorty chose Victoria because of its friendly familiarity. He had to pick on one of the two so as not to seem too unusual.

'Aye, Victoria. Aye. Let's see now.' The man hesitated, then the words came with a rush. 'Take a trackless.'

'A what?'

'A trackless. A trackless car. Didn't you ever hear of trackless cars. They've done away wi' tram lines now.

They've got trolley cars, trackless they call them.'

'Okay, which one and where does it stop?'

The man told him. Shorty hurried on to catch up Molly.

'Okay, kid, stop by that lamppost and take the same trolley bus as me. Go up on top and book to Victoria Station.'

He gave her the instructions in passing and walked on to stand alone by the lamppost. There was nobody else on the top deck of their car and, when the conductor had taken their fares, Shorty leant across the aisle and gave Molly more instructions and a pound note.

'When you get to the station, find out where the next train is going and book two tickets. I'll stay outside. Then they won't tie up that the bloke who asked where the station was bought a ticket to wherever the hell it is. Come out. Give me my ticket and we'll go in separate. You can get in the same compartment as me. Billo.'

A couple of youths came up to the top deck and sat behind Shorty. One of them looked at Molly with a hunter's eye, saw that her stockings were torn and her coat splashed with mud and had no further interest.

At the station Shorty lurked outside in the covered approach and looked at bills advertising excursion trips to Skegness and Cromer. When Molly came out again his casual saunter could not conceal the eagerness he really felt.

'Okay? Where d'ya get them for?'

'Grantham. Here's your'n. Cop.'

She handed him his ticket and he looked at it in the dim light, twisting it in his fingers.

'Grantham? Blimey, that's on the Great North Bloody Road, ain't it? It was just about there the bastards first got on my tail.' He laughed. 'Well, skip it. We can always get out at some station before Grantham. What time's the train start?'

'Ten minutes. Platform 4.'

'Okay. Good gel. Go on ahead. I'll tail you up slowly. Go in the Ladies' Waiting Room.'

He waited for a minute and looked around. Nobody seemed to have rumbled him, so he wandered slowly into the station, showed his ticket to the collector and crossed the iron footbridge. There were three or four people in the General Waiting Room, so he did not risk sitting by the much-coveted fire, but strolled up and down the platform.

He'd made a dopey break, flashing himself about the joint like this. Much better to have waited outside and dived for the rattler at the last minute. Ah well. Couldn't be helped now, least said, soonest mended. This wasn't half a big station and all.

He looked at the tin advertising plates and the enormous red-brick walls that reached up to the Victoria Hotel.

A train came in.

'This the Grantham train, mate?'

'Aye.'

He put his hand on the smeary brass of the door catch and let himself into the first vacant third smoker that he saw. He let down the window so that Molly could pick him out and with a sigh sat down and stared at the pictures of Alnwick Castle, Crowle and Immingham Docks. Even before Molly arrived he managed to get a whiff of the familiar over-heated, steam-smelling air.

She hopped in just before the train left. They were the only passengers in the compartment. Shorty pulled up the window, grinned at her and said: 'Well, Moll. We beat them to it that time, kid.'

'We sure did. Got anything to smoke?'

'You betcha.'

He copied her imitated American accent and, tossing her his cigarettes and a box of matches, stood up swaying and grinning. The train was running bumpity-bump unevenly over the points outside the station. Molly lit a cigarette and grinned back at him.

'Come on, sit down. There's no extra charge.'

She patted the seat beside her. He sat down, put an arm comfortably round her waist and even more comfortably rested his feet on the seat opposite. He could feel the warmth of Molly's body as she leant against him.

'Gi's a fag, ducks.'

She lit a cigarette from the end of hers and passed it to him.

'Ta. You're not a bad kid you know.'

Shut here in the box-like third-class compartment he felt happily secluded from the cares and pursuits of the outside world. The train beat rhythmically on through the night. Raindrops smeared the outside, cigarette smoke bleared the inside, of the closed windows.

'You're not so bad yourself.'

He laughed happily and pulled her a little closer towards him. Molly frowned a little in thought.

'Shorty,' she began.

'Yes?' He turned his face to hers anxiously, troubled by the doubt in her voice. 'What's up?'

'You know what I said about Alice, well I take it all back. You're all right. You'd never do such a thing. Never in all your natural born days. I'm sorry I didn't believe what you was telling me.'

'That's all right, kid.'

He kissed her.

'That's the first time I've kissed you since we got together last night.'

She shook her head.

'Blige me. You ain't half a Mr Forgetful and no mistake. You kissed me before you went and screwed that chat.'

'Caw. So I did. Well, 'tain't going to be the last.'

He kissed her again, and again. His lips, his hands

were urgent. She returned his caresses, then pushed him away.

'Look out, people'll see.'

'Who?'

'People living by the line. Don't forget there's lights.'

'All right, all right. I'll fix that.'

He pulled down the blinds on each window. It felt even more cosy than ever. Blimey, it was as snug as a flowery where they had locked you up for the night.

He sat down beside her and kissed her again, but her mood had changed.

If that wasn't tarts for you all the world over. Do your best to please them and then they go and change their minds. No getting to the bottom of them. Not a chance of it.

Fiercely he pulled her to him and kissed her. He could smell the drying mud on her coat, it excited him. After all he had fought for her. Surely he was entitled to his corner if anybody was. She responded weakly and then protested.

'Don't.'

'Why not?'

'I'm tired. You don't know what I bin through. Wait till we get to the hotel.'

'Oh blimey. Come on. Have a heart.'

'No.' She took his arm and put it round her waist. 'Go on. Sit comfy. Like a gentleman.'

'Blimey, bloody fine rye mush I'd make.'

'Well, you're as good as the next man, ain't you. Got nothing to be ashamed of.'

'Caw. You're right there and all, kid. Right enough. 'Tain't my fault if Alice goes and gets done in, is it? I served me sentence for what I done and if that ain't fair enough, I'd like to know what is. Straight up I would. Once they get a bloke down, they won't let him up on his scotch pegs again and that's a fact.'

'Yerce. Same across. I'm in the same boat as you and all. What chance I got? How'm I ever going to go straight?'

'Them days was all right round the Edgware when we was chavvies, wasn't they?'

'Not arf.'

'Best days I ever had. Caw. You don't half see some ups and downs when you come to weigh it up. If I had my life over again, Gorblimey, I dunno.'

'Funny, ain't it?'

'Funny? You got a nice sense of humour, I must say. What the evening papers call Cockney Wit. Caw. I ain't a-kidding to you. Just you send that stroke in and they give you half-guinea. Funny? You can call it funny, but I don't. Where's the fun come in in being chased all over bloody England with the papers and the radio and all that caper on your tail? Funny? Caw. I'd rather be in the nick, doing half a stretch. Caw, what wouldn't I give to've lost about six days' remission! Funny? Blimey.'

He stared moodily in front of him. She played with the fingers of his hand which rested on her hip.

'Here, tell you something, kid. If I get on my feet again, beat this rap or something, how's about us tying up together?'

'Watchew mean? Tallying along? Going case and working the knock-off two-handed?'

'Garn. Don't talk so soft. Ain't you never bin to the pictures? Don't you know what romance is? I'm arsting you to marry me and you do no more you turn round and start talking about the crook.'

'Arsting me to marry you?'

'Blimey. You heard. Got cloth ears or something?'

'Me? Caw. What you want to marry me for?'

He swallowed hard.

'Oh, dunno. You ain't such a bad kid. Good little mucker-in. I must love you, I suppose.'

'Ow, Shorty.'

She slid her arm round his neck and kissed him all over the face. He kissed her back, not hotly or frenziedly, but with slow, comfortable affection.

She whispered in his ear.

'D'you love me? Reelly?'

'Yes. I reckon I do.'

'Go on. Say it.'

'All right. I'll say it then.' There was more than a hint of despair in his voice. 'I love you.'

'Ow, Shorty, I love you too. I do ever so. When I found out you'd nicked a police car last night, when you went and done that gaff, I said to myself, "That's the bloke for me. He's dead game," I said. "That's the bloke for me. None of these poncefied blokes," I said, "nothing of that sort about him. And he ain't a mug neither," I said. "Real wide boy," I said. "Wideo, that's what he is. Wide as Regent Street that's what he is." And then s'afternoon when I read that piece they put in the paper, you know, that bit about you and poor Alice, why I could of cried my eyes out. Proper browned off with life I felt. And then you go carrying on about me shopping you.'

She sniffed. He patted her cheek.

'All right,' he said gruffly. 'Skip it.'

'And then you come along and set about them geezers on the toby. Made me think a bit. Ow, Shorty.'

'That's all right, kid. That's all right. Soon as I'm out of this mess we'll settle down. I'll even take a job and go straight. There! How about that? Give up everything for you I will. Get a barrow and see if I can't pick up something that way.'

'How're you going to get out of this mess? Ever think of that? Watchew going to do? Be on the run all the rest of your natural life?'

'I'll get abroad somewhere and send for you.'

'Don't talk daft. You got to work out a plan.'

'Nuts. I've had about enough of working out plans. Let's enjoy life a bit.'

'Billo. Train's stopping.'

A porter was calling out the name of the station, but neither of them could understand what he was shouting.

The train hissed as it stood by the platform. A man opened the carriage door, peered at them, and walked away again.

'What's oop? Having a bit of love wi'blinds drew?'

Both of them flashed him sickly shy grins. Shorty belched.

'I could do with something to eat.'

'Get something at the next stop.'

'Yerce.'

The train started again. Shorty put his hand on Molly's shoulder and looked at her. A pulse was twitching in his cheek.

'No, dear. You got to get things sorted out.'

'Cops have got me sorted out all right and all.'

Molly stared, with her watery blue eyes, at the picture of Alnwick Castle. Her legs were scratched and sore. For a moment she was too weary to go on with the argument. Shorty whistled and stroked her hair.

'Here,' she said suddenly, trying a new line of attack. 'Watchew going to do about me?'

'Watchew mean, what am I going to do about you?'

'Yerce, watchew going to do about me? You want to study me a bit and all. It's all very well for you. You don't seem to mind having a game of hide and seek. Where do I come in?'

'Well, if you don't like it you can do the other thing. They're always saying this is a free country. We ain't married yet or nothing. You can sling your hook any time you feel like it.'

'Supposing I don't want to? Ever stop and think about that? Suppose I want to settle down? Entitled to settle down, ain't I? You say you love me, don't you?'

'Course I do, kid, you know that. How many more times d'you want me to say it? You want to get that gramophone record, you know, the one that sounds as if it got stuck at one place.'

'All right, all right. No need to take me up like that. You're a regular Mr Sharp. It's a wonder you don't cut yourself. No,' she pushed his hand away. 'Stop it. I don't like it. I told you I was tired, didn't I?'

She gave it up in despair. The new line of attack was as valueless as the former. Suddenly an idea came to her. This ought to do the trick.

'Here,' she said, 'what'd you give for another chance? Start again fresh and all that caper? Millions of bloody pounds, wouldn't you? Well, you won't get no fresh starts with this,' she paused, 'this hanging over your head.'

''Tain't my fault.'

'I didn't say it was, stupid. If you got away somewhere and I got away and all and you had this hanging over . . .'

'Don't keep on saying hanging.'

She laughed nervously.

'Well, if you had this, if you was scared all the time that some flatty would be coming along to knock you off any minute, nice mess you'd be in never able to settle down to nothing nor me nor any of our kids, if we had any, neither.'

'Something in that,' Shorty grudged.

'You believe in luck, don't you? How can you expect to have any luck when you don't give it a chanst to come along up your street? How can you try to prove you're innocent if you keep on running away all the time? Yellow, that's what you are. Yellow.'

'Nark it. I ain't yellow and you know it. Look what I done to them two.'

'I know all about that, but you're scared of giving yourself a chanst to show you're not guilty. Listen, I'll make a bet with you. If you go and give yourself up you'll stand a good chance of creeping with it. Blokes have got chucked before.'

'You're a right one, you are.' He drew away from her in horror as though she were a reptile. 'Want to get me hanged, you do.'

'Oh blimey.' She had lost her temper. 'Don't talk silly. I'm trying to help you, you berk. Give yourself up. Box clever and I expect you'll creep. Don't see why you shouldn't. And then you'll be able to go straight and no hard feelings. I'll go straight and all while you're waiting trial. Get a job or something and then when you come out, stone me blind, will we have a good time.'

Her voice rose in an enthusiasm that began to affect him.

'There's something in what you say,' he said dubiously.

'Course there is. Caw, we'll wipe the slate clean, we won't owe nobody nothing and then . . .'

'And then you woke up. Supposing I get topped.'

'You won't get topped. Not this trip out. Not likely. Not if you do like what I said. The longer you're on the run, the sooner they'll think you're guilty. Give yourself up somewhere and you'll beat the rap.'

'Think so?'

'Course, I think so.'

'All right, even if I do I'll have a bloody good meal first. They half starve you to death at them police stations. Bread and marge and a cup o' tea and lucky to get it. That's all it is.'

Molly put her hand out and took his. She knew now that she would have to make a very bad mistake to lose the battle. He shifted along the seat and sat with his body against hers again. She fondled his face.

'We'll have ever such a nice time, dear. I'll get a job and save a bit o' money while you're on trial and start getting a bit of a home together and then . . .'

'Sounds all right.'

The train drew into a station and pulled up with a jerk.

'Let's get out here,' said Molly.

Shorty stood up. There was a sinking feeling in his heart as he leant over to open the door.

'P'raps we'll be able to get them two sheiks nicked and all if we do it this way. Pity we don't know their names.'

She patted his arm.

'Caw, wouldn't that be a bit of all right?'

'Well, I'll have a tightener first. Don't want to starve meself. I got me health and strength to think of same as anybody else.'

She kissed him lightly on the lips and jumped down on to the platform.

'Do what you like, dear, I'm with you. You know that.'

CHAPTER XX

'Well, ready yet?' He had not quite finished chewing his bacon sandwich.

'Yerce. I'm ready,' said Alf, getting up and pushing back his chair.

'Okay. Let's get going. What's your name, Tom, Dick, Bill, Bert or Jim?'

'Alf.'

'Mine's Wally. Well, come on Alf. So long.'

'So long, mate. G'luck, Alf.'

Bill still sat on in the café while the other two walked across the mud in the darkness to Wally's lorry.

'Leyland, ain't it?'

'Yerce. What'd you use to drive?'

'Same. Nice job to drive even if the windows in the cab was broken.'

'Yerce, they're all right.'

Wally, picking his teeth with a match-stalk, walked round the lorry, kicking at the tyres and occasionally feeling a knot of the ropes that held the tarpaulin down.

'Lousy night to drive.'

'Proper bastard. Ain't left off for twenty-four hours. Your mate's going to cop a packet if he's going north across the moors. Be a cowson between Carlisle and Moffat.'

'You're telling me.'

'Ah well, better get going I s'pose.'

With the match still between his teeth Wally started the engine.

'Have a cup of tea round about Colsterworth or Stretton,

that's what we'll do. Another at Biggleswade and we ought to be in the Smoke round eight or nine tomorrow morning. I'll fiddle the log sheets to make it come right, any road.'

He swung himself up into the cab.

Alf crouched in his corner. Anyway this was more comfortable than the old tub he used to drive. Hell of a lot better. Nothing like having plenty of glass in your cab and not having the draught blowing through.

He stuck his hands deep into his pockets, and settled his feet more comfortably.

This old-timer drove all right too, even if he was a bit of a big mouth. Nasty night to be driving and all. Caw, it was funny to be sitting in the cab doing nothing just like a bloke who was taking a wagon leap. When he'd been a van boy, first job he'd ever had, he used to sit in the lorry all day, at the back though. Lots of drivers used to have mates when he had first come on the road. It used to be the natural thing in them days before they brought the Act in. One bloke driving, another kipping. Kipping in a lorry wasn't much cop. Different now you had to stop; so the firms cut down on expenses and only had one bloke on the lorry.

He sighed.

Be tough if he couldn't get another job. Going and signing on, sitting around, three-penny seats at the pictures in the afternoon, wondering if you had enough dough to take your tart out, laying around caffs for hours on end scratching yourself.

Kipping in a lorry wasn't much cop.

He began to doze off. His head nodded, his chin sank on to his chest. In the atmosphere of petrol fumes, cigarette smoke, lubrication oil and sacking he slept.

He was awakened by a tug at his sleeve. He shook his head, blinked his eyes and sat up with a start. His mouth was dry, his head ached, his neck was cricked and he felt lousy. Wally was tugging at his sleeve.

'Come on, dozy, wake up. You wasn't half having a nice little kip.'

'What's up? Where are we?'

'Just passed through Tuxford.'

'Caw. Made good time and all.'

Wally laughed and drew on the cigarette that he was smoking so that the tip glowed a momentary red in the darkness.

'Lot you know about that. You bin to bye-bye all the time and you looked so nice there in dreamland that I felt I'd have a basin and all myself just to see whether it was as good as it looked.'

'Okay. You want me to take over?'

'No. I want you to have a game of last across. Come on. Hop over the engine. Got your licence? Just in case anything goes wrong.'

'Ar.'

'Know this road?'

'Wouldn't think so. I only bin on it the last three or four years. That's all.'

'All right, come on, change over.'

They clambered over the engine and changed places. Alf peered through the wet windscreen that the wiper ineffectively cleaned and felt with his feet.

'All right,' said Wally. 'Let's go. What are we waiting for? You said you knew Leylands.'

Alf drove in darkness along the familiar road. Just past Tuxford, eh? After Tuxford came that bit of a bypass round Carlton-on-Trent, then Newark.

Gawd almighty it was just, well not far anyway from here that there'd been that nice little turn-out last night. Just like in the fourpenny bloods he'd used to read when he was a spiv: 'Little did our hero think when last he passed this way.' He looked round so that he could pass this witticism on to Wally, but he was sleeping.

Even in the darkness Alf could see his white face, with the bristly, unshaven lower jaw drooping beneath the open mouth.

He peered ahead at the road again.

Better keep his mind on the job and drive good. Maybe this bloke had a bit of a drag with his firm and might be able to work him in somehow. Anyway, he didn't want him to turn round and say, 'Well, you wasn't no loss when you got the belt. Call yourself a driver?'

Although he would have liked a cup of tea, the after effects of sleep were rapidly leaving him. His mouth felt dirty, but his eyes were clear enough. If it hadn't been for that crick in the back of his neck he would be feeling swell.

Carlton-on-Trent, Newark, Balderton, Long Bennington. The well-known villages, on the well-known road, with the well-known flat fields of eastern England. The slow, lumbering miles were eaten up one after the other by the southbound wheels of his lorry. Then there was that bit of a bypass round Foston.

Which way did Wally take that?

He glanced at him, but he still slept on.

Right fork was best.

He was driving well now. All his self-confidence was restored. Every now and then he passed another lorry and, in passing, leant out of his cab with his tight thumb in the air just to show that he was making out all right. He hummed as he drove, first 'Little Old Lady', then the 'Wheel Of The Wagon Is Broken'.

Oh, so the wheel of the wagon was broken and it ain't going to turn no more. That was just where they were wrong. It was going on turning. He was a good driver all right and he'd get another job quick enough.

He drove through Great Gonerby a little faster than was necessary. The wagon swayed a little before he pulled it out into the straight again.

How fast could the old bitch travel anyway? Probably better than the Leylands he was used to. Well, it depended on the load. Anyway have a go, boy. Try and see.

He let it rip. Coming towards him was a big white Fairclough's lorry with a trailer. There was only just room for them to pass each other with a swoosh. Exhilarated he leant once more out of the cab and triumphantly gave the high sign.

Windy bastard, he didn't half looked scared, that driver. Blokes like him didn't want to be on the road at all if they couldn't take it.

Christ. Christ almighty.

Behind, immediately behind the lorry he had just passed was another. It had pulled out a little into the road so that the driver could see past the leviathan in front of him.

Oh God. Could he do it?

They were roaring into each other. With an enormous wrench Alf tried to pull the wheel over. Wally woke with a jerk.

'Gawd.'

It was too late. Alf left go of the wheel and shielded his head with crossed arms like a boxer against the ropes in a corner. He was icy calm. It was the end. He knew it.

There was a crash as the two monsters collided. For half a second, a half-second that could not be measured, everything was still, then, as if by an afterthought the other lorry turned slew-wise across the road, the load behind crashing on to the cab.

Sick and frightened Alf watched with his mouth open. He sat there. He went on sitting there. Wally shook him.

'Blimey,' he said, 'you've done it now. Lost me my job and all.'

'Your hand's bleeding. You must have put it through the glass.'

'Never mind my hand,' Wally was wrapping a handkerchief round it and tying a knot with the help of his teeth. 'Never mind that. Let's go and have a dekko at the other geezer.'

They got down from the cab. Alf's legs were made of rubber. He could not walk across to where the load of sacks of potatoes from Wisbech *en route* to Nottingham lay scattered all over the road. He vomited. Wally came round the cab.

'Come on, son,' he clapped him on the back. 'Pull yourself together. You want to be all right before the slops are here. That there radiator ain't half dinged. It's copped a beauty and no mistake. Come on.'

He put his arm round Alf's shoulder and steered him across the road. Painfully the other driver was climbing down.

'Caw,' he said, 'that's done it. Christ.'

He put a hand on the small of his back and then fell, first to his knees, then on his face.

'He ain't dead, is he?'

Alf's voice was like a little boy's. Wally looked at him with mingled fury and tenderness.

'Don't talk silly. Just got a wrench, that's all. P'raps a rib gone.'

He knelt down on the road beside the driver and ran his hands over him.

'Where's it hurt you, mate?'

'In the gut and on the back. I copped the wheel in the gut. The missus won't half rort. I'll lose me job for this, you mark my words. I only got started last month. Been out eleven munce.'

'You won't lose your job,' Alf burst in. 'My fault.'

'Here, less of that. You'll get us all in a nice mess, you will. Insurance don't cover you. I might creep on this. Here, gi's hand.'

Alf helped Wally pick up the other driver and sit him on a sack of potatoes with his back resting against a wheel.

'Listen chum,' said Wally. 'If we stick together we're out of this. We got into a skid, see? You was behind another wagon what's gone on and we don't know the number. Just an accident all round. Nobody's fault. What speed was you going?'

He looked at Alf who hung his head.

'Gawd knows. I don't. I let her right out.'

'Well, you're a right berk, you are. There's one of them secret clocks in the wagon and just as soon as there's an accident they'll take it down and have a butcher's at it. Gawd knows what to do for the best. Here. Here comes a private.'

He held up a hand and signalled to an oncoming private driver to stop. The driver could have done nothing else. The lorries blocked the road.

'Excuse me, mister. There's bin a bit of accident. Could you take this geezer into a doctor's?'

'Sure.' He opened the door at the back. 'Lift him in.'

Wally and Alf helped the other driver into the back seat.

'All right, son, you'll be okay. Use your nut, that's all. It's my fault. It'll take the rap.' He looked at the private driver. 'You better send the cops out and all.'

'Right.'

He put his car into reverse and tried to turn in the narrow road. Wally and Alf stood watching him, with the contempt of experts burning in their eyes. As soon as he had managed the job, Wally spoke.

'Now, dopey, you take a ball of chalk. I might be able

to get the old tub going and I might not. You've lorst your job and I reckon you've lorst me mine. So take your hook out of it. I don't want to see no more of you. Bloody danger, that's all you are.'

Alf turned silently southwards.

CHAPTER XXI

Shorty came out of the café with Molly. His stomach was full of warm food. He ought to have been feeling better, but fear spoiled all that.

They walked along arm-in-arm. Nobody would think that they were lovers taking an evening stroll, for their faces were too set, too white, their movements and gestures too fixed. In spite of the contact of their bodies a blanket of constraint was between them. There was a lot to say, but neither of them dared to talk.

Few lights were burning in the shop windows. For some time past the public houses had turned out their customers and stood darkly inhospitable beside the roads. As they passed the green Shorty looked longingly across the road to the cinema. He had not been to the pictures since he had come out. Not once. Not unless you counted that visit to the News Theatre.

There was nothing like being at the pictures, in the dark, looking at the screen, listening. Nothing like it for taking your mind off things. You couldn't beat it. He maybe wouldn't go to the pictures again.

Molly looked at him, and squeezed his arm. He gave no response. She tried to smile brightly.

'I got a good mind not to go through with it.'

'Go on. Don't be dopey. You know it's all for the best.'

'Better be.'

'Course it is.'

'If it ain't you've done me in same as that bloke done in Alice. If it is I needn't 've gone tearing all over England.'

'There's the nick.'

She pointed across towards the police station. Shorty's heart sank. His legs faltered.

'Let's walk just a bit down the road first. Well, I don't want to go in. Not yet.'

'Come on.'

She tightened her grip on his arm and propelled him into the station. A constable looked through a window at them. His face seemed enormous, but friendly. Shorty's tongue was stuck to the roof of his mouth. He could not speak. Molly nudged him in the ribs.

'Yes? What do you want? Looking for digs or something? Lost anything?'

'I don't want anything off of you, but you want me, I reckon.'

Shorty's voice seemed to him to be coming from a long way off. The grin which he tried to put on would not quite happen. The constable lost his friendly look.

'What's up? Who are you?'

'I'm Mathews.'

Shorty's weariness was unbearable. He blinked his hot gritty eyes and leant his hand on the window ledge. The constable took a year, it seemed, to speak again.

'Mathews? The Drummond Street murderer? Who's the young lady? What's she doing here?'

'You'll find that out later.'

Molly's voice was acid. She and the police were not friends. The constable pushed the door open and was in the passage. His blue figure towered over Shorty. He had hold of his wrist.

'Albert Mathews,' he was saying, 'I am a police officer and I am taking you into custody on a charge . . .'

Neither of his listeners heard the familiar words. Their minds were elsewhere.

'. . . warn you that anything you say may be taken down in writing and used as evidence at your trial.'

'You got the wrong man. You're making a mistake.'

Shorty's customary answer broke in on the provincial policeman's dream of fame and promotion arising from a sensational arrest.

'What d'you mean? You said you were Mathews.'

'Yes, but I didn't do it.'

'All right, all right. We'll go into that later. This way please.' He led him down the corridor towards the cells. 'You wait here, Miss. There's one or two questions I want to ask you.'

Molly stood there shifting her feet. The old smell of police stations, of cold stone floors, boots, metal polish, ink, brass, soap and paper was making her frightened. The impersonal green walls were closing in on her. In the distance she heard a cell door clang. If she didn't sit down soon she would faint. She tried resting her back against the wall.

From a long way off she could hear two pairs of footsteps. They drew nearer. Squeaky boots. The constable was back again with his superior.

'Well, Miss,' his voice was comfortably middle-aged but businesslike, 'you seem to have got yourself mixed up in a funny business. If you don't mind stepping in here . . .'

He opened a door leading into a barely-furnished office. Immediately she was inside she sat down on a hard Windsor chair, her body sagging like a sack of potatoes that had been slumped down in the corner of a barn. She was conscious of his gaze running over her. It was not the usual stare which she was professionally used to, but the cold hard look of an expert trying to put her in a category.

The police officer cleared his throat.

'Your name, please?'

She told him.

'Address?'

'No fixed abode.'

He raised his eyebrows, but made no comment.

'Occupation?'

'Waitress.'

'Ha, I suppose that means the usual thing.' He cleared his throat again. 'Waitress, domestic servant, dance instructress, actress, it's always one of those that you girls say.'

'What are you getting at?'

He smiled with slight coyness.

'Come on, there's a good girl. Why'nt you own up?'

'Well, if this ain't the very latest.' Molly's voice rang with all the indignation of which she was capable. 'Here's me coming into a police station to make a charge against somebody and you start leading off at me, insulting me. I'll tell the magistrate about this, so help me, and he'll have something to say, you mark my words. He'll have something to say?'

'What is all this?' The officer scratched his head. 'Why don't you say what you're come here about?'

'You never give me a chance. You just started firing off questions at me and insulting me.'

'Well, tell the story in your own words.'

The officer was now badly rattled even if he did not show it. Molly looked down. She was trying to whip up her weary brain into action. For the moment she had the enemy at a disadvantage and her sharp metropolitan brain knew it.

'I was assaulted by a couple of men who tried to – er – make me do something when I was rescued by that gentleman.'

'Which gentleman?'

'The one you just locked up.'

'Ah,' he smiled benignly. 'You mean the prisoner Mathews? Tell me the circumstances of the assault.'

'Well, they knocked me about terrible. Look at the state I'm in.'

She held out her coat and stuck forward her feet and legs for his inspection.

'Yes, yes, I can see that. But where did this take place? How did it?'

'Now you've got me, Mister. Somewhere between Sheffield and Nottingham. I don't know their names.'

'Well, I'm afraid that's outside our jurisdiction. If you like to make a charge I'll put through a call to the police forces concerned, but you've got to give me a few more details first. How did you come to be there?'

'They picked me up in their car. They were gutter-crawling. I went for a ride with them, but I didn't know what they were going to do. They set about me when I refused to give in . . .'

'And you were rescued by the Drummond Street murderer? Now, that story doesn't wash. You're trying to cover up for him. Where did you meet him?'

'He was coming along the road . . .'

'Yes, in a stolen police car. He picked you up in a café last night. Yes, you might as well look scared. You've got every reason to. You're either an accessory after the fact or else you've committed the misdemeanour of misprision of felony. It all depends.'

'Don't talk wet. As soon as I found out you was after him I put him up to giving himself up. Do you think he'd 've come here if it hadn't been for me?'

'Oh, you did, did you?' The officer's manner changed. 'Oh, you did. Well, that's different. You done right there. Tell me what you know about it.'

'He didn't do it. He went to see her and she was done in already, so he gets scared and scarpers.'

'That's his story. He's got to make the judge believe that and he's going to have quite a job. Ah well, that's nothing to do with me. It's a job he's got to work out him-self. What's all this about the assault? You'd better tell me.'

Molly told him the whole story. He rubbed his nose.

'Well, you'll have a job to convict if you can even get them arrested. I'll call the police in Nottingham and Sheffield and see what they can do. You've helped us. I'd like to help you. What you going to do now?'

'Have a kip. I'm worn out. I'll go to that place at the end of the town where they let rooms cheap. I'll be there if you want me.'

She got up. He got up too and stood there looking fatherly. Molly made a hesitant, half-hearted movement towards the door.

'Better be going, I suppose,' she mumbled. 'Goodbye.'

'Good night. Thank you.'

He sat down again. Molly stood with her hand on the door knob. The brass felt smooth and cold under her rough, red palm.

'I reckon,' she said in a weak, inconfident voice, 'there's not much chance of him getting off, is there?'

The officer looked up with troubled eyes. Somehow she disturbed his official equanimity and his complaisance in his despicable job.

'Well, that's up to the jury. If they believe his story . . .'

'You'll treat him right, won't you?' she pleaded. 'Don't bash him about.'

'A call's been put through to Scotland Yard. They'll be sending an escort for him directly. That's all.'

'Ow, I do hope I didn't make him do wrong.'

Her snivel turned into a sob. She held the back of her hands up to her eyes and ran from the room. The officer sat on the table. He was thinking. Suddenly he lit a cigarette and jumped to his feet. He crossed the passage to the charge room.

'Bring me Mathews to my room,' he commanded. 'Come in yourself in ten minutes.'

In a few minutes Shorty shuffled into the room. He stared around with defensive belligerence.

'Won't even let a bloke have a kip.'

'Sit down.'

Shorty sat down.

'Listen. You might as well come clean. I've been running the rule over that tart of yours and she's come the copper.'

Shorty stared up at the ceiling. He was too old a hand to be taken in by that old trick. With the fingers of his right hand he drummed on the edge of the table. The officer tried again.

'You done right,' he said, 'coming and giving yourself up like this. It'll count for you at your trial. The Yard are sending up an escort to fetch you. If you make a statement I'll hand it over to them and that'll count in your favour and all.'

All the time that the officer was speaking Shorty went on drumming. Again he changed his tactics.

'If you do me a good turn,' he said, 'I'll do one for you too. It'll be a big thing for me if you let me have a nice little statement to turn over to the Yard and I'll see to it that they don't mix it for you.'

Still Shorty's fingers drummed the same old tune. The town clown looked at him savagely.

'Sulky, eh?'

'No, just wide.'

'Oh, you're one of the clever boys, eh? Not so clever that you didn't make some silly mistakes. You left your dabs all over the gaff, you know.'

He drew his chair a little closer. 'Stop that damned tapping.'

For a short while there was silence.

'So damn smart,' he said, 'you went and killed a poor girl. Why'd you do it?'

'I didn't.'

'Killed a girl just for the few shillings she had. I don't call that wide. How much dough did you get?'

'I didn't get anything.'

'Killed a poor girl and you got no money out of it. Come on. I can't swallow that. You don't expect me to stand for that old madam, do you? Blimey. You just said you were wide. Well, I suppose you know best. If you didn't do it for money, why did you do it at all?'

'Listen,' Shorty had lost his temper, 'you bone-headed, flat-footed, numbskull of a bastard country copper . . .'

'Don't you start calling me that. You'll regret it . . .'

'. . . I didn't kill her.' Shorty's voice ended in a screech.

'All right,' the officer was looking around anxiously, 'if you won't help yourself, you won't. You're just being a mug to yourself. Caw, I don't half pity you when them bogeys from the Yard gets hold of you.'

The door opened. Another policeman was standing inside the room. As Shorty turned his head to look, the questioning officer gave the newcomer a nod and a wink.

In three strides he was beside Shorty's chair.

'So you're the bloke that pitches into policemen and steals their cars!'

He hit him hard on the cheek with his open hand. Shorty's already aching head rang. He swayed to the right and jarred his ribs against the edge of the table. His heart felt sick. Long ago he had learnt what it felt like to have a policeman's boot in his stomach.

'Get up.'

Shorty dully obeyed. The newcomer had two red spots of excitement and artificially-created anger blazing in his cheeks. Unknown to himself his mouth was twitching. Shorty stared at him sullenly.

His brain snapped. He was accused of a murder he had not committed, he had been chivvied about England for two days, and now he was going to be beaten up. Well, nuts, he'd give as good as he got.

With a roar he sprang at his tall enemy throwing back his head so that he butted him in the jaw. They both fell on the floor, rolling over and over in an effort to get a hold. The policeman grabbed at Shorty's throat, but he put on an arm lock that made him wish he had not. The questioner, for all his belly and forty years, joined in the fun. His boots squeaked as he stooped and pulled Shorty off his comrade.

In his arms Shorty struggled and bit and kicked, but the other policeman was now off the floor with his uniform covered in dust.

'Now you murdering little bastard, I'm going to half kill you. I'd finish you off if it wasn't for the hangman. I'm going to leave you just so much alive that he'll have something to work on. That's all.'

Shorty managed to bring up one of his heels. With a gasp his holder let go. He ducked his head and rammed it straight into the other's stomach. Even if he was going to be killed he was going down fighting.

Again they rolled on the floor, but this time the policeman's superior weight told. In a minute he had on a half nelson. With his disengaged hand Shorty beat on the floor like an all-in wrestler who was giving up.

'All right, get up.'

He yanked Shorty to his feet and coldly and methodically set about him. In a few seconds Shorty sagged limply on to the floor. At a sign from the other policeman his assailant stopped work and lifted him on to a chair.

'Now. Are you going to make a statement?'

Through his cracked lips Shorty whispered a defiant 'No'.

CHAPTER XXII

How brightly the lights were dancing in the rain, how beautifully the black road glistened, how smooth and subtle were the lighted limousines. How shabby was the raincoat that he was wearing and how hairy were the bony knees beneath his threadbare trousers.

So what?

Even if that were true, still at his behest one man was a fugitive from justice, another was locked in a police-station cell, one woman lay dead in her flat and another on a slab in a mortuary awaiting the findings of an adjourned coroner's jury.

Ha! What was the world? How ignorant it was of its own self.

Swinging his arms he walked back towards Piccadilly.

A man could be despised, wear shabby clothes, eat insufficient and repugnant food, women might despise him and scorn him unless he paid them money, the world might refuse to employ him, exploit him when it condescended to hire his labours, yet he could ruin the life of four of his fellow humans. Power was nice. Everyone could have power if only they bothered to accept it.

It was wonderful. The world was the best thing that had happened. Death. There was a joke. Death sublime? What nonsense, death was as sordid and as furtive as life. There was no dignity in life, no pomp in death.

'Come on, hurry up. Make up your mind.'

A taxi driver shouted at him as he stood trying to make up his mind to cross the road to his bus stop.

He did not mind. He was ecstatic. He stood there

enjoying the idea of the sordidness of power, the power of sordidness. A passer-by jostled him.

'Come on, Dad. Want all the street? Think you've bought the bleeding road or something?'

Good heavens, the impudence of the urchin behaving like that.

His rapture vanished. Once again he was just a drab little man, very much aware of his own insignificance. It became imperative for him to assert himself once more. He turned and walked back in the direction in which he had come.

Those policemen thought they were clever. He would go and taunt them. The Lone Wolf would show his mastery over their bovine stupidity.

With his mouth working and little bits of saliva bubbling at the corners of his blackened lips he hurried towards the station.

Marvellous. This was going to be the master stroke. Bearding the police like lions in their own den, taunting them, tantalizing them, pitting his brains against them only to escape their clutches.

His weak spindly legs trembled as he walked, his heels felt bruised every time that they came in contact with the pavement.

What a marvellous story this would make. Dick Turpin, Jack Shepherd, Robin Hood, Arsène Lupin, Ultus, Dr Fu-Manchu, the Clutching Hand! Pooh, they were only amateurs, the rawest beginners compared with the Cleansing Flame. He would write it and make his fortune.

His heart sank a little while he thought of the piles of rubbishy paper in the top drawer of the shiny yellow chest-of-drawers with china handles, in his bed-sitting room. How many stories had he started with high hopes, but never finished?

He was still thinking of china handles when the constable on duty asked him his business.

'I understand, officer,' his tone was lofty as befitted an important man, 'that you have in custody the man who murdered the unfortunate woman of the streets – Pauline?'

'Oh, you do, do you?' The constable looked at him mockingly. 'And what's that to you?'

'I would be interested to hear whether you have also arrested the man Mathews wanted for the murder of another woman of the same type, who, I believe, resided somewhere in the neighbourhood of Euston Station.'

'Here, what's the game? Watchew getting at?'

'My good man, that is not the way to address me. I am one of the public. You are a public servant.'

'You get out of here, wasting my time.'

Obediently he turned to go. Suddenly he swung round with a leer on his lined grey face. He sidled, fawning, up to the constable.

'Is there any chance of my seeing this man?'

'Here, what's up with you?' The policeman seized his arm, not sure whether to run him out of the place or not. 'You been drinking? I'll poke you inside if you don't watch out.'

'No, no, don't do that. I wouldn't like that.'

His manner had changed to an abject cringe.

'Well, what's all this stuff about murder? You been to the pictures once too often I reckon.'

The policeman stood there holding the man's arm, not quite sure what to do. At last he said: 'Sit down in here a minute, old man. I might be able to do something for you.'

Docilely the man sat in the Charge Room while the constable went across and knocked on a door marked CID. He went in. Three officers were running the rule over Big Harry who looked badly scared.

'Excuse me, sir,' the constable said, 'there's a man outside who seems to have heard something about this business.' He nodded significantly towards Harry. 'He may be a bit touched in the head, but it seems funny that he's got on to it so soon.'

'Okay. Bring him in. He may know something.' The officer turned to Harry again. 'Now, Harry boy. Use your loaf. How'd you know that your Pauline had picked up some queer-looking steamer?'

'Queenie give me the office.'

'Why'd she do that?'

'Well, she thought he was a funny-looking bloke and she hadn't seen Pauline for some time.'

'Why'd she tell you?'

'How'd I know?'

'Come on, Harry, tell the truth. Was it because she knew that you and Pauline were cased up?'

'Look here, guv'nor. Tell me this? Can you do me for living on the earnings of someone who's dead?'

'I don't know. I don't suppose so.'

'Well, yes then. That's why.'

The door opened again. The constable came in with the man in a raincoat. All four occupants of the room looked at him strangely.

'Here he is, sir.'

'Okay. What's your name?'

'Er. Walter Hoover.'

A light leapt into Harry's eyes.

'He's the bloke. I lay you five nicker he is.'

'Seen him before?'

'Never.'

'All right, officer. Take Harry along and lock him up. I'll be seeing you soon, Harry. Sit down, Mr Hoover, and tell us all about it.'

Rather bewildered, Walter Hoover sat down.

He was glad to be resting. After all he had had a very tiring evening.

'Now tell us all about it.'

'Er. All about what?'

This was all rather difficult. He was not quite sure what was happening. The lights were so bright. Who were all these men anyway? He sat there with his little mild eyes open widely and cleared his throat nervously.

'Why you murdered her?'

'Oh, you know I did. How on earth did you find out? Which one do you mean, Pauline or Alice?'

'Who's Alice?' The detective inspector was smiling.

'The girl who was murdered in Drummond Street.'

'Oh, so you killed Alice, too.'

'Yes, yes, of course, I thought you knew.'

He fluttered with his hands as if to make an excuse for bothering them with such trivialities. It was a pity that there were no china knobs in the room. How strange it was that one should find such very pleasant people here. They were so knowledgeable, weren't they? And in a police station of all places. He wondered who they were.

The detective turned to his colleagues, made a grimace, and shrugged his shoulders. When he looked at Walter again the expression of his face was tolerant and kindly.

'Take my advice, Walter,' he said, 'run along home. You'll get yourself into trouble one of these days if you go around talking about having done murders. There's a law against wasting the time of the police. It's called committing a public mischief.'

Walter got up from his chair. He looked around the room and at the faces of the other men with sudden interest. So they were plain-clothes policemen. Detectives. How interesting. Just like Lestrade in the Sherlock Holmes stories. What a narrow escape!

'Just a minute, sir.'

'Yes, Edwards.'

'I've got an idea. May I try it?'

'Yes. If it doesn't waste too much time. What is it?'

'May I go now?'

'No, Walter.' It was Edwards who was speaking. 'Sit down a minute. You see, sir,' he was whispering in the guv'nor's ear, 'I've got an idea that he's not just the usual nutty bastard who's kidding himself that he's done the job. How about sending an officer along with Harry to bring in that girl Queenie, while I just ask him a question or two? It won't do any harm.'

'Sure. That's not bad. Go on, Young. You take Harry. And make it snappy.'

'How many other girls have you killed, Walter?' asked Edwards.

'Oh, none. None.'

'Why did you kill Pauline?'

'I didn't. I swear I didn't.'

Sweat began to pour down Walter's face.

CHAPTER XXIII

Young unlocked Harry's cell.

'Come on, Harry, we're taking a little walk.'

Suspiciously Harry cowered against the white-tiled wall. What were they up to now? Never trust bogeys.

'It's all right. Keep your shirt on. I just want you to come and help me get that girl Queenie.'

Harry stroked his moustache and stared at the detective, trying to read from his face what it was all about. He sat down again on the wooden shelf that served as a bed.

'No, no. Blimey no. Nick me if you like. Top me if you like, but I'm not going to come the copper on nobody. Help you to lift Queenie? Caw, you must have done your nut.'

Young leant against the door jam with one leg crossed over the other.

'Don't be berkish. I ain't going to lift Queenie. I want to get her to identify this bloke they've got in the CID room. He may be the funny-looking bastard who Queenie saw.'

'Ow.' Dubiously Harry picked up his hat and put it on at its usual leary angle. 'But suppose the word goes round I put the finger on this geezer. Right cowson, I'd look.'

'I don't understand you, blimey if I do. Pauline was your girl and you won't lift a finger to get the geezer that creased her. You won't even try to help yourself out of a jam.'

'Yerce, but helping the slops. You know how it is, mate. You'll get me a bad name all over the West End.'

'Come on. We'll go in a cab. Nobody'll see you.'

'All right, all right, but I can't say I like it. It looks bad.'

'Where's she likely to be?'

'Anywhere from Piccadilly corner of Bond Street to about halfway down Burlington Gardens. It's too early for her to be on the Dilly itself and she never gets around Sackville Street.'

'Come on. Let's go.'

Harry sat in the cab, looking out of the window as it cruised slowly along. He didn't like this job at all. Funny bloody business whatever way you looked at it. Proper turn-out. Funny kind of a night all round. Tough on Pauline kicking off like that. She'd been a good girl and all. He'd have all the work of making another girl. Still that wasn't so bad. A bloke could get a bit of fun out of that at times.

'There she is.'

'Where?'

'That fair-haired tart. The tall one next to the tart with a dog.'

The detective leant forward and tapped on the glass that separated them from the driver.

'Okay, taxi,' he said. 'Wait a bit. Now, Harry, do your stuff. I'll trust you not to do any vanishing tricks. I'll wait here in the cab for you.'

Harry got out of the cab and sauntered towards the girls. His composed air hid a very frightened man. Queenie wasn't such a bad-looking brass at that. He wouldn't mind tallying up with her and that Charley of hers wasn't much cop. It ought to be easy enough to get her away from him.

'Oy, Queenie.'

'Yerce?' She came up to him. 'Blimey, it's you, Harry. Heard about your Pauline?'

'Not half. It's her I want to chat you about. Remember that funny-looking geezer you reckon you seen?'

'Yerce, I seen him again and all – on the Dilly. Don't half give me a turn. All the girls is scared out of their lives. Thinking about turning in the game and going home. Lousy night and all.'

'Could you pick him out and all?'

'Shouldn't wonder. Why?'

'Werl,' Harry became embarrassed. This was going to be harder even than he had thought. 'You see the bogeys lifted me. Tried to hang the job on me, they did. Well, I've told them about this bloke you've seen and, you see, well it's like this, they want you to come down and identify another geezer they've got who might be him. Blimey, Queenie, it's not my fault. I'm not turning into a copper or nothing. It's either him or me. Don't get me wrong.'

'I'll identify the bastard all right if it's him.' Queenie laughed shortly and bitterly. 'Deserves to be topped, as if we girls didn't have it hard enough without some murderous cowson coming and making it all the worse. I don't like no flat-foots myself, but I'll help them get anyone of that sort. Topping's too good for him. That's what I say.'

'Okay. Come along then, darling.' He took her arm. 'There's a bogey in that cab.'

'Riding in cabs with a bogey! That's a stroke to come out with! Caw, I won't half giggle about this with the girls.'

Queenie sat in the middle of the back seat of the taxi. She pressed outwards with both knees. It was fun trying to give a kick to a ponce and a policeman at the same time. She was sorry the ride was so short.

When they had arrived at the station she and Harry waited while Young went into the CID room. He came out with the detectives.

'Okay, Harry. You can scram now. We don't want you no more. Just keep your nose clean, lay off the girls and we'll lay off of you.'

'So long, Queenie.'

'So long, Harry. Remember what the nice detective said.'

'Up yours.'

Harry hurried away. He sure was glad to be doing it. The senior detective spoke to Queenie.

'H'm, h'm. So you're Queenie, are you? And a nice little dish you are.' He eyed her up and down, but she returned his look with as bold a stare as his. He dropped his gaze. 'Ah, well, to business. My business I mean, honey, not yours, although I wouldn't say no to that if I was pressed. Come along.' He took her arm. 'I want you to try to pick out the man whom you saw getting into a taxi with Pauline.'

He led her into a long, empty passageway. Ten men were standing lined up against the wall, with a uniformed constable on guard at each end of the line. None of them, she noticed, were wearing hats or raincoats.

She walked rapidly up and down the line. She recognized him at once. It would have been quite easy for anyone to have picked him out, for he was the only one whose face was grey and frightened, whose muscles were fixed in fear. His eyes were darting from left to right. She went straight up to him and laid a finger on his chest. He shivered a little at the impact and looked straight at her.

Dirty little cow, flouncing her body in front of all these men. Pauline, Alice, and her.

His eyes widened, he sprang forward. Before he could reach her, a man on either side had seized his arms.

'That's him,' said Queenie.

A detective went up to him.

'Walter Hoover, I am a police officer and I am taking you into custody on a charge of wilfully murdering Pauline . . .'

'No, no, no. You can't, you mustn't. You don't understand. I was telling lies. Besides, I'm the Master Mind. You're only the police.'

'Come on, come on, come on. Less of that.'

The uniformed constables had hold of his arms and were taking him off to the cells. The detective smiled at the prostitute.

'Thanks, Queenie. We'll want you some time. You'll have to give evidence. You give us your name and address and we'll let you know. We won't need you tomorrow morning. It'll be only formal evidence.'

She gave him a card from her bag. It was gilt-edged.

'This is what I always give my best clients. Come up and see me sometime.'

'Okay.' He laughed. 'Any reduction for friends?'

'You're no friend of mine, sonny boy, no friend of mine. Goodbye.'

'So long. Be good.'

'Same to you.'

She strolled off, swinging her bag, conscious of all the eyes that followed her.

CHAPTER XXIV

Shorty awakened with a start from his troubled sleep. He ran his fingers up the smooth glazed tiles of the wall.

Oh, yes. He was in that rural nick. Blimey, he was thirsty. He swung his legs over on to the ground and tried to stand up. A sharp pain caught him in the ribs and he collapsed, gasping, on to the blankets. One thing was certain anyway. They had given him a right going over.

He lay huddled on the wooden ledge and listening to the sounds of protest and steps coming down the corridor.

'Shut up you. Get inside that cell and keep quiet.'

'Watchew locking me up for? I ain't done nothing. Can't a bloke be walking about the streets in this town?'

Some poor bastard done for suspect. London bloke and all. Probably some poor old cowson off the frog and toad. He'd heard that voice before somewhere. Ah well, make a bit of company in the nick.

'Get inside there. You'll pipe down if you know what's good for you. The bloke next door can tell you what happens to people who cut up.'

There was the sound of slithering feet on a stone floor. A bump as the body careered into the cell and a clang as the door was shut.

With his hand softly stroking his battered face, Shorty lay there and waited until the footsteps had died away. There came another clang as the door separating the corridor from the remainder of the police station was slammed.

Carefully he got off his bed and went to his door.

Good. They had not slammed the shutter to.

Resting his head against the cool metal of the door Shorty started speaking: 'Oy, mate.'

He heard the other man groping around.

'Oy, mate. This is the bloke in the next cell talking. Come up to your door and we'll have a chat. You there yet?'

'Yerce, here I am.'

'What they nick you for?'

'Gawd knows. I was just walking around and they grabs me. Ask me what I'm doing out after midnight, and whether I live in the town, and when I say no they float me along here.'

'Ah. They'll charge you with loitering with intent to commit a felony. You'll get anything up to three months.'

'Think so?'

'Think so. I'm bleeding sure. Suspect is one of the raps you can't beat. Got any fags on you?'

'No. They searched me and took my fags and money.'

'Well, I got some. Here, cop. Stick your hand out of the shutter and reach out to the right. Got it? Okay. Got a match? No? Well, here's three of them and all. These blokes up this way always use them red-tips.'

'Thanks, mate, you're a toff.'

For a little while they smoked in silence. The cigarette was hurting Shorty's sore mouth, but he was enjoying his blow all the same. It helped to keep his mind off things.

His neighbour spoke.

'What they pinch you for?'

'Me? Well, you see,' somehow Shorty felt very diffident about what he had to say. 'I mean, you see they said I done a murder.'

'A murder? Blimey.'

Again there was silence. Then the other spoke again. His voice was a mixture of horror and interest.

'Here, mate,' he said. 'You ain't that bloke Mathews, are you?'

'Yes. That's me.'

'Remember me?'

'Well, your voice is kind of familiar but I can't say I do.'

'I'm Alf. That bloke who give you a ride on a lorry last night. If it wasn't for you, you bastard, I wouldn't be here now. I lorst me job all because of you. I hope you're satisfied.'

''Tain't my fault. Besides, you're a bloody sight better off than me. Suspect's oxo. I could do three months on me tochas. How'd you like to be hung? Parse and analyse that one.'

'Yerce, but I never bin in trouble before, well not what you'd call trouble. I did get brought up to the Juvenile Court when I was a spiv for knocking off apples from a barrow, but now you gorn and ruined me life for me. Gawd knows what the old lady'll say. First I go and lose me job, then I land in gaol.'

'Go on. Don't take on so. You might get chucked.'

'What's chucked.'

'Acquitted. If you use your nut you might touch lucky. Got any money?'

'A bit. Why?'

'Well, I'll tell you what to do then. Listen. You'll have to go inside for a week on remand, but that's better than getting a carpet . . .'

'What's a carpet?'

'Three months. Besides, once you've got a conviction you're marked for life. Look at me. I got five previous. You want to use your loaf, you might get out of this little lot. Tomorrow morning when the bench is weighing you off say, "please, Your Worship". Don't forget that. Call the poxy old bastard "Your Worship". He's bound to be a miserable old cowson and likes to wop it in, so if you call him "Your Worship" he'll feel pleased with himself. That's what they call psychology. So say "please Your Worship may I be remanded for a week in custody? I don't want to spend seven days in prison, but I would like time to obtain legal aid".'

'Yes. How do I get that?'

Alf's voice was eager now. Shorty was the expert. Last night he could have told him all about driving lorries: tonight he had to keep still and listen.

'Well, you have to box a bit clever. The police are certain to suggest a mouthpiece, a lawyer that is, for you, but don't you stand for that. They'll get you some dopey old punk who they want to do a favour for. Make an application to see the Probation Officer and ask him to give you the name of a good 'un. Don't you look at any of them shysters the police try to palm off on you. Tell the lawyer the whole story, get him to write to your firm for a character and if you're lucky you'll creep. Know any parsons or doctors who'll speak for you?'

'No. Can't say's I do.'

'Didn't you never belong to a boys' club or nothing when you was a nipper? You must of.'

'Well, yes I did, come to that.'

'Live at home in the same district?'

'No. There was one of them housing schemes and me old man got work as a night watchman at a factory and we moved out to one of them new estates.'

'That spoils the boys' club. Well, never mind, get your mouthpiece to put in a bit about the old man. You know the kind of stuff. "So trusted and respected is the family that his father is actually in a position of considerable responsibility." I reckon you'll be all right. Billo. Lay down, there's the screw coming.'

A heavy-footed policeman came down the corridor, glanced into the cells and walked away. When it was all quiet again Alf spoke: 'What'd he want?'

'It's me. You see when a bloke's in on a serious charge

like I am they have to come and take a butcher's at him every so often just to see whether he's done himself in or not. I just thought of something. They charged you yet – you know, said that bit of madam about "I am a police officer and I am taking you into custody" and all that caper?'

'No. They just arst me where I lived and where I worked and then poked me in here.'

'Well, you stand a chance then. They're probably on the blower now trying to check up on you. If what you told them is true they'll very likely turn you loose.'

'Think so?' In his excitement, 'Caw, I don't half hope you're right. Bastard dump to be in this.'

'You wait till you're in a proper nick. Then you'll learn all about what it means.'

'What are they like?'

'Well, the cells *are* a bit better than this, but all the same it's one of the places you want to keep out of and I ain't a-kidding to you. It ain't so bad for me, because I got used to it, but you wouldn't like it.'

'What's the grub like?'

'Bloody murder.'

'Do they bash you around at all?'

'Yes, if you give them half a chance but they ain't so bad as these bastard coppers who're so nice and kind on the street and then knock spots off you when they get you inside. They give me a right doing. It's all a matter of getting used to it inside. Still, whatever way you look at it, it's a bastard. You know what they say, don't you?

> Stone walls do not a prison make,
> (He began to recite with mockery)
> Nor iron bars a cage.
> A poet in another age,
> Wrote this inspiration.

The stone and bars they use today,
Make a damn good imitation.'

Alf laughed. Once again they fell silent. Shorty lit another cigarette. He limped up to his cell window, then limped back to the door again. Would Molly wait for him? Don't talk silly, of course she would. If she hadn't thought a lot of him she wouldn't have talked him into giving himself up.

'Here, mate,' he said. 'You got a tart?'

'Yerce. I was sweating on getting married this Whitsun but now I reckon it's just about mucked up, me out of work and all.'

'Well, you'll see what kind of a jane she is. If she sticks by you when you're in the nick you're all right. She's a good tart. If she don't, well, blimey, you're well rid of her. What kind of a tart was she? Nice looking?'

'Smashing. Caw, mate, you'd be surprised. If she goes and gives me the bullet I don't know what I'll do. Cry my bleeding eyes out and go stark staring raving mad I expect. Lovely dish she is. Think the bloody world of her.'

Locked up in their cells, prevented from seeing each other, lonely and in the darkness both of them had lost all shyness.

'I got a tart and all. I don't suppose you'd call her much cop, but she's all right for me. Girl in a million. She'll stand by me all right whatever happens, even if they, well you know.'

'What about that other girl? You know the one you done in.'

'I never done her in.'

'What happened then? I was reading a piece they put in the paper all about you and that bride.'

'If I was to tell you, you'd be just as wide as me. I'll give you a bit of advice. When you get to the nick you keep a still tongue in your head. Lots of blokes have talked themselves into no end of bloody trouble. I've seen them nicked at the gate just because they opened their mouths a little too wide when they was in stir. Besides, how'd I know the cops didn't put you in next door to me just to get me talking. They're wide enough to do that and I'm wide enough to know it.'

'All right, all right. No offence.'

'That's all right. Only I got to look out for myself. Here. Want another fag? Cop. You got them colneys still?'

He passed Alf over a cigarette as a peace offering. Before he had given himself up he had taken the precaution of buying himself a packet of twenty. Alf lit up and then spoke again. He could not keep the curiosity out of his voice.

'Reckon you'll get off?' he asked.

'Well, I got a sporting chance. Never say die. They'll never kill me anyway.'

'Whatchew mean?'

'Well, it's this way. Supposing the worst comes to the bloody worst and they find me guilty and I don't get me sentence commuted. Well, here's the set-up. The last morning comes. They stand me on the trap, and stick the old rope round my neck. Well, all I got to do is weigh up when the topper's likely to get to work and give a jump into the air. Well, down I come on Sweet Fanny Adams and break me bleeding neck. It's me who's killed myself. They ain't done it. I got that satisfaction.'

'I see.'

'Terribly bloody things hangings. The bloke hardly ever comes off and dies clean. Either the weight of his body wrenches his nut right off or he slowly strangles to death. And all the air's kept pinned up in his lungs. A couple of screws, warders that is, goes down into the pit and cuts the rope and all the air comes out like a scream. You can hear it all over the stir.'

'You been inside when they been hanging someone?'

Alf was biting his nails in his morbid excitement. Never before had he been given first-hand information like this. Caw, it'd make his old man's hair curl when he told him.

'Have I been inside? Blimey, I wish I had a quid for every geezer they've topped while I been doing bird. You can hear the drop go crash and all the boys kick up a bawling and screaming and banging. It's just like the Zoo. And the day before you can hear them testing it. The condemned man can hear it and all.'

'Blimey.'

'Yes, it's a bastard for him all right. And the hangman comes in his cell the day before and measures him and weighs him just to see what sort of drop's needed, and all the time two screws are holding his arms so that he doesn't set about the cowson. Caw, the things I could tell you. Once, when I was a cleaner in the Ville I got ordered to scrub out the execution cell.'

'What'd you do?'

'Said I wouldn't. You're entitled to. You ought to see the laundry in Wandsworth. They call it the slaughterhouse because that's where they have the floggings. You have to scrub the floors after. There's blood and bits of skin all over the place. The screw that does the actual bashing gets a tip just like a waiter. I seen blokes' backs afterwards. You got to see it to believe it and then you get bigheads writing to the papers saying that flogging ought to be brought in for this, that, and the other. I'd like them to have a basinful. The bastards.'

'Gawd strewth.'

'You may well say that. You don't know what you're bloody well up against until you get in one of them places. Once I seen a bloke stick his head inside a lavatory pan.'

'Caw, why?'

'The screws were bashing him over the nut with their

keys and that was the only place he could put it out of harm's way. Billo, there's someone opening the passage door.'

Shorty waddled back to his bench again. He could hear keys jangling. Well, that meant someone was going to be opened up. He hoped it was Alf. He couldn't stand any more himself if they were going to take him out and do him again.

The steps paused outside Alf's cell.

'Alfred Smith?'

'Yes.'

'Well, we're letting you out of here, Alf. We checked up on you and you're all right. So get out. Only don't let us catch you hanging about this town.' He opened the door. 'Go on. Muck off. Get your property at the office.'

He slammed the door. Shorty heard Alf scampering away down the passage. He had not even bothered to say 'So long', or wish him luck. The constable was peering through into his cell.

'Albert Mathews?'

'Watchew want?'

Shorty did not get up from his bed. His heart was heavy. He knew that his aching body could stand no more blows.

'We've had a call through from the Yard about you. As regards that murder you've been charged with, you're in the clear. They've got a bloke.'

'Yes?'

Forgetful of his aches and pains Shorty leapt happily towards the door.

'Then I can get out of here. Caw blimey. Where'd my tart go? I got to go and tell her this. Got the right bloke. Well, that's a bit of all right, I must say.'

'Just a minute, please. Just a minute. There are a couple of other charges you've got to answer. Burglariously breaking and entering a house near Bawtry last night, violently resisting lawful custody, and driving away a car without the consent of its lawful owners, the Lincolnshire Constabulary. Would you like to make a statement?'

'Nuts. Let me kip.'

He rolled over in his blankets.

Well, he was over the worst anyway.

CHAPTER XXV

Shorty walked along in front of the warder. He was smiling. It was nice not to have to be working in the shoe shop that day. As they crossed the exercise ground he looked up at the sky. It was the clear, metallic blue that only comes on sunny winter days.

The warder unlocked the iron-barred gate and Shorty passed into the reception room. He rubbed his chin with his hand. It was a pity that he couldn't get a shave.

'One on, sir.'

His landing officer handed him over to the reception screw, who sat at a desk with a sheet of paper in front of him.

'Albert Mathews? 6134, cell location B.3.27.'

'Yes, sir.'

'Give me your cell badge.'

Shorty unbuttoned it from the breast pocket of his coat and handed it over to the screw.

'Well, Mathews, you're the only discharge this morning. An officer will escort you. What are you trying to smuggle out. Turn out your pocket.'

Shorty took out the blue handkerchief that looked like a duster, a small piece of red carbolic soap and three sheets of toilet paper that had to last him till the end of the week. The officer got up and ran practised hands over him to see whether he was carrying any contraband.

'Okay,' he said, 'the cleaner will give you your breakfast and a bit of bread and bully for your dinner. Go and sit on that bench.'

Shorty went over and sat down at the end of the bench

so that he could rest his back against the wall. His face and eyes wore the furtive, patient look that is common to all prisoners.

The three reception cleaners came in. One of them had a red band on his arm to show that he was on parole not to escape and so was allowed to walk about the prison without escort.

'Only one discharge this morning,' said the screw. 'Give this bloke his grub and get him his clobber. 6134, Albert Mathews, cell location B.3.27.'

One of the cleaners came across to Shorty with a half-pint of porridge, a pint of tea, eight ounces of bread and half an ounce of margarine.

'Here y'are, mate. Get stuck into that if you want it. The red band'll get your clobber and poke it in one of them floweries.'

He pointed towards a row of cells.

'Blimey,' said Shorty, 'bit of all right this. Three blokes waiting on one. Couldn't get served better at a cook shop.'

He picked up his spoon and started on his porridge.

'Oy, mate,' the cleaner recoiled in horror. 'Blimey, you ain't going to eat that, are you? I never known a bloke eat his burgoo on the morning he's going out before.'

'Take it easy, son, I'm only going out to give evidence at the Assizes against a couple of blokes. I got another nine months to do here.'

'What they get done for?'

'Indecent assault.'

'Reckon they'll get chucked?'

'Bleeding well hope not. It was my tart and all they set about.'

''Spect to see her up at the Court?'

'Yerce. She's promised to send me in hot dinner. None of them bully sandwiches for me. Preserved meat, eight ounces. Caw.'

'Waiting for you, this bride? Well, she must be a good kid. My piece scarpered with another geezer before I been in here six weeks.'

Shorty took a big gulp of the dreary prison tea.

'What screw's going to be my escort, d'you know? Hope it isn't Wallsy, or the Grey Ghost. Now Grackerjack and Harper, they're real boys. Let a bloke have a spit and a drag I shouldn't wonder.'

'Yeah. Don't forget if your tart works you some fags, work them to me as soon as you come in tonight before you change back into stir clobber. I'll give you back half of whatever you get.'

'Okay.'

'How long you doing?'

For a miracle the cleaner had managed to maintain quite a long prison conversation without bringing this question into it before.

'Stretch. Well, two concurrent stretches. But you want to see the list of previous I got. Caw, you'd think I was Crippen or somebody like that.'

'Here, ain't you the bloke that went out before to give evidence in a murder trial? Against that bloke what-a-name, you know, the geezer that they reckoned had done his nut?'

'Hoover. Yerce, that's me.'

'Blimey, you ought to be ashamed of yourself, straight up you ought. Doing time and all and you going giving evidence for the prosecution uphill and down bloody dale like that.'

Shorty put down his plate and mug.

'Why?' he asked. 'What about that other bloke that give evidence against Hoover. Doing half a stretch for poncing on another girl he was too when they drag him out to say how he found this piece Pauline murdered. Besides, I'm quitting the crooked lark. I'm going straight as soon as I'm out of here.'

'Yeah? That's what they all say.'

'Here, chum,' the red band was shouting, 'your clobber's in that first flowery. Get into it. Leave your stir clothes in it.'

Shorty got up and walked across to the cell.

Maybe he was being a bastard putting the finger on these blokes. Well, it was every man for himself. They'd tried to have him done. Besides, it wasn't as if they was a couple of the boys. Straight guys they'd been. Wrong side of the counter. Serve them right to get caught out.

Nuts.

AFTERWORD

For an author whose literary legacy is so firmly embedded in the 1930s it is salutary to acknowledge that James Curtis did not die until 1977. While his characters dodged around grimy, monochrome London with upturned collars, belted raincoats and trilby hats like a furtive version of the man in the Strand cigarette advert, Curtis was more likely to have encountered youths with orange Johnny Rotten hair and ripped tee-shirts adorned with safety pins as he walked the streets of North London in that final year of his life. Lester Piggott romped home in the Derby on a horse called The Minstrel, Virginia Wade won the ladies singles at Wimbledon and the throbbing disco beat of Donna Summer's 'I Feel Love' floated out of open pub doors in that hot, sticky summer.

He was living in the Kilburn area in a sparsely furnished bedsit. He had not had a book published in 20 years and any royalty cheques from his early work would by then have been few and far between. The London-Irish crowd he drank with would have had no idea that their friend Jimmy had been a best-selling author and once had the moguls of the British film industry beating a path to his door. Curtis would not have told them because fame and fortune were never his goals or his god. As the series of letters from 1974 (reproduced here) demonstrate, he remained principled and unbending to the end. The prospect of hard cash and a possible revival of interest in his work was not enough to tempt the financially straitened pensioner to allow others to take liberties with his fiction. A company called Raintree had taken an option to film *The Gilt Kid*, and the first letter is from Curtis Clark, one of the producers, explaining the inevitable delays in getting the film moving. The second is Curtis's draft response to seeing the screenplay that had been developed. The third letter is from the partner of Clark (who was a friend) making an attempt to build bridges, and the final letter is from James Curtis to his agent. The letters and an angrily annotated screenplay were about the only items relating to Curtis's lifetime of work found in his bedsit following his death. Sadly, or happily – depending on which way you look at it – those bridges were never constructed.

Dear James

My plans to make the picture certainly haven't changed. The main factor delaying proceedings is selecting the director. Since mid January the screenplay has been with John Boorman (director of *Point Blank*, *Deliverance* and *Yardboy*) who as yet, due to various reasons, hasn't read it.

I have an arrangement to produce the film through VPS-Goodtimes in conjunction with David Puttnam. This means that VPS-Goodtimes will act as production company and Puttnam will secure the necessary deals in the USA to finance it. But all this hangs on the director at the moment. Failing Boorman we plan to try Losey, who is probably even better suited to the project.

Once a director is selected all else should begin to fall into place. The changes that should be made to the screenplay will best be made after a director has been selected, especially since the directors we have in mind are all good screenwriters and will no doubt want to effect some form of contribution depending of course on which one in the end directs.

Curtis Clark

May 1974

Dear Curtis

Subject: *The Gilt Kid* screenplay

This version is just as infantile and badly constructed as I had feared. Not only has all characterization and authenticity been thrown to the winds but also a crass ignorance of the customary rules of dramaturgy is displayed. The story originally was about certain individuals in London's underworld; the central character has now become an Italian Old Etonian.

I suggest the title be changed to *Bedborough's Revenge**. If you want to give the Gilt Kid his comeuppance, this should surely be contrived by a personage involved in the main part of the story.

It would seem that the two main causes of the story being off kilter are:

(1) Arbitrarily updating the period from 1934 to 1936, when in England the worst part of the Depression was over.
(2) Unnecessarily building up all that nonsense about the Mayfair party, which is improbable, has nothing to do with the story and merely holds up the action in an excruciatingly boring fashion. There are 22 pages of it.

Here are several widely inaccurate improbabilities:

(1) A deportee is either repatriated on a ship of the host

---

* A character from the book, but Curtis may have borrowed the name from George Bedborough, a London bookseller who was prosecuted in 1898 at the Old Bailey for selling literature dealing with homosexuality.

country or else he is released and would have been sent home in a British ship. In the latter case, he is not in custody. The second method is used when a man is extradited, when, of course, he would be kept under surveillance. Note I have checked on this.

(2) There is no need for that *Boy's Own Paper* tosh about exporting arms to Italy. At that period it could have been done quite legitimately.

(3) An elementary error in dramatic construction is the way those Mafia characters are dragged in at the heel of the hunt. They should have been established earlier, and the audience is entitled to recognize them. Furthermore, the so-called Sabini mob from Clerkenwell in the 30s were Anti-Fascist and, though of Italian parentage, were thoroughly Cockney in speech and behaviour. They operated mainly round the Races and Dog tracks. The only organized gang of Mediterranean heavies at that time was the Maltese Mob from Stepney.

I have marginally inserted certain emendations of dialogue, etc, in order to make it either smoother or more realistic until I got fed up with doing it.

By all means go ahead and make the picture with the story as it stands, but don't expect me to waste more time and energy over something by which I am thoroughly turned off.

James Curtis

1974

Dear James

Just a little note – as I hear there has been some disagreement about the script?

Anyway I wondered, all that aside, if you would have a drink one evening in Soho with me, since I am hoping that our friendship will withstand any of these business aggravations – also I would like to hear from you the various thoughts and feelings you have on *The Gilt Kid*.

Please phone me at work or at home if you will have a drink with me.

Looking forward to hearing from you,

Yours,

Penny Clark

August 1974

Dear [blank on draft but believed to have been to his agent]

Thank you for your letter dated 27 Sep 1974. It would seem that Curtis Clark intends to go ahead with the screenplay** as it is and yet expects me to be technical advisor on the production. That of course is quite out of the question. He cannot lay that sort of an each-way wager which places me in an intolerable position. It would be impossible to get any authenticity with a production which is ridiculous in concept and amateurish in construction. Furthermore, I would not wish to have my name associated with any farrago such as they envisage. Let him make the picture, if he can, but let him realize I want nothing further to do with it.

** The screenwriter was Richard Marquand who went on to direct *Star Wars: Return Of The Jedi*.

The nervous strain of trying to convince him that the whole atmosphere reeks of petit bourgeois fancifulness would be too much for me.

I had supposed that this was already clear to him.

James Curtis

September 1974

LONDON CLASSICS

THE GILT KID

JAMES CURTIS

The Gilt Kid is fresh out of prison, a burglar with communist
sympathies who isn't thinking about rehabilitation. Society is
unfair and he wants some cash in his pocket and a place to live,
and he quickly lines up a couple of burglaries in the London
suburbs. But complications arise, and he finds himself dodging
the police, checking the newspapers and looking over his
shoulder, fearing the ultimate punishment for a crime he
hasn't committed. He remains defiant throughout, right up
until the book's final, ironic conclusion.

James Curtis recreates the excitement of 1930s London as he
delves into the sleazy glamour of the underworld mindset; a world
of low-level criminals and prostitutes. His vibrant use of slang is
as snappy as anything around today, his dialogue cosh-like as the
Gilt Kid moves through the pubs and clubs and caffs of Soho.
Curtis knew his subject matter, and this cult novel doubles as
a powerful social observation.

This new edition comes with an introduction by Paul Willetts,
author of *Fear And Loathing In Fitzrovia*, the best-selling
biography of author Julian Maclaren-Ross, and an interview with
Curtis's daughter, Nicolette Edwards.

London Books
£11.99 hardback
ISBN 978-0-9551851-2-0
www.london-books.co.uk

London Classics

NIGHT AND THE CITY

GERALD KERSH

Harry Fabian is a cockney wide boy who will do anything for
a pound note; a storyteller who craves recognition, his endless
lies hiding a deeper, inner weakness. He is also a ponce, and
one who is walking on the edge. It is only a matter of time
before he topples over the side.

Set in 1930s London, against a fluorescent West End backdrop,
Night And The City brings the Soho of legend to life, the streets
a tangle of drinking dens and night-clubs, author Gerald Kersh's
characters flamboyant creations who add a cosmopolitan edge to
the book's journey into the darker shades of human nature.

Twice filmed, *Night And The City* remains a 'lowlife' classic,
and comes with an introduction by John King, author of
The Football Factory and *Human Punk*.

London Books
£11.99 hardback
ISBN 978-0-9551851-3-7
www.london-books.co.uk

LONDON CLASSICS

A START IN LIFE

ALAN SILLITOE

Alan Sillitoe's first novel, *Saturday Night And Sunday Morning*,
was published in 1958, *The Loneliness Of The Long-Distance Runner*
arriving the following year. Both were hits and led to high-profile
films, which is turn cemented his reputation. Tagged an
'Angry Young Man' by the media, Sillitoe's ability to record
and interpret the lives of ordinary people was nothing short of
revolutionary. He has been prolific ever since and remains one of
England's greatest contemporary authors.

A Start In Life tells the story of Michael Cullen, who abandons
his pregnant girlfriend and heads 'to the lollipop-metropolis of
London in the 1960s'. Cullen is, in theory, leaving his problems
behind, but he is 'the Devil on two sticks' and becomes involved in
a smuggling ring with Moggerhanger, a man who believes 'that
you must get anything you want no matter at what cost to others'.
Cullen is an optimist, with an eye for the ladies, but his new
swinging lifestyle is soon under threat.

Includes an introduction by DJ Taylor

London Books
£11.99 hardback
ISBN 978-0-9551851-1-3
www.london-books.co.uk

London Classics

WIDE BOYS NEVER WORK

ROBERT WESTERBY

Young Jim Bankley yearns to leave behind the production line
in a provincial town when he chances on a London razor-gang
at a local dog track. Seduced by the opportunity to live life on the
edge, he follows them back to London. He is thrown into a milieu
of bruisers, brasses, car dealers and con-merchants. Drenched
in sleaze and brutality, he begins to wonder if the simple
life is so bad after all.

Robert Westerby's 1937 novel provoked a stir at the time,
authentically lifting the lid on an underworld metropolis that
many pretended did not exist. It has lost none of its punch in the
ensuing 70 years – and slang historians generally credit Westerby
with coining the term wide boy. The book was filmed in 1956
under the name *Soho Incident*.

This new edition boasts a penetrative introduction from leading
London author and broadcaster Iain Sinclair, whose work
includes *London Orbital* and *London, City Of Disappearances*. He
is a long-time champion of often overlooked vintage London
writers such as Westerby, James Curtis and Gerald Kersh.

London Books
£11.99 hardback
ISBN 978-0-9551851-5-1
www.london-books.co.uk

LONDON BOOKS

FLYING THE FLAG FOR
FREE-THINKING LITERATURE

www.london-books.co.uk

PLEASE VISIT OUR WEBSITE FOR

- Current and forthcoming books
  - Author and title profiles
- A lively, interactive message board
  - Events and news
  - Secure on-line bookshop
  - Recommendations and links
- An alternative view of London literature

IAIN SINCLAIR

HACKNEY, THAT ROSE-RED EMPIRE

Once an Arcadian suburb of grand houses, orchards and conservatories, Hackney declined into a zone of asylums, hospitals and dirty industry. Persistently revived, reinvented, betrayed, it has become a symbol of inner-city chaos, crime and poverty. Now, the Olympics, a final attempt to clamp down on a renegade spirit, seeks to complete the process: erasure disguised as 'progress'.

In this 'documentary fiction', Sinclair meets a cast of the dispossessed, including writers, photographers, bomb-makers and market traders. Legends of tunnels, Hollow Earth theories and the notorious Mole Man are unearthed. He uncovers traces of those who passed through Hackney: Lenin and Stalin, novelists Joseph Conrad and Samuel Richardson, film-makers Orson Welles and Jean-Luc Godard, Tony Blair beginning his political career, even a Baader-Meinhof urban guerrilla on the run. And he tells his own story: of forty years in one house in Hackney, of marriage, children, strange encounters and deaths.

Praise for Iain Sinclair:

'Sentence for sentence, there is no more interesting writer at work in English' *Daily Telegraph*

'He is incapable of writing a dull paragraph' *Scotland on Sunday*

'Sinclair is a genius' *GQ*

read more

IAIN SINCLAIR

WHITE CHAPPELL, SCARLET TRACINGS

Following the fading fortunes of a predatory clutch of ragged book dealers scavenging for wealth and meaning amongst the city's hidden tomes, *White Chappell, Scarlet Tracings* reveals a present-day London rooted in a dark and resonant past. The chance discovery of a dust-torn classic is hailed as a triumph, but within its battered covers lie uneasy clues to the century-old riddle of the Whitechapel murders.

Part biography, part mystery, part exorcism, *White Chappell, Scarlet Tracings* explores the occult relationship between fiction and history and examines how their bloody collision has given birth to the London of today.

'A sane, darkly brilliant report from the back streets of knowledge and power'
New Statesman

'Extraordinary . . . ruined and ruthless dandies appear and disappear through a phantasmagoria interspersed with occult conjurings and reflections on the nature of fiction and history' *Guardian*

'A Gothickly entitled guidebook to the abyss . . . burns with radioactive energy'
London Review of Books

NORTH SOHO 999
A True Story Of Gangs And Gun-Crime In 1940s London

PAUL WILLETTS

Just before 2:30pm on 29 April 1947, three masked gunmen entered a shop in Soho. Little did they realise that they were about to take part in the climax to the unprecedented crime wave afflicting post-war Britain. *North Soho 999* is a vivid, non-fiction police procedural, focusing on what would become one of the twentieth-century's biggest and most ingenious murder investigations – an investigation which later inspired *The Blue Lamp*, starring Dirk Bogarde.

'A brilliant snapshot of '40s London, peopled by crooks, coppers and creeps. Willetts slices through time with the skill of a razor-flashing wide boy. Essential reading' – John King

Dewi Lewis Publishing
£9.99 paperback
ISBN 978-1-904587-45-3
www.dewilewispublishing.com

THE GORSE TRILOGY

The West Pier / Mr Stimpson And Mr Gorse / Unknown Assailant

PATRICK HAMILTON

In Ernest Ralph Gorse, Patrick Hamilton creates one of
fiction's most captivating anti-heroes, whose heartlessness and
lack of scruples are matched only by the inventiveness and
panache with which he swindles his victims. With great deftness
and precision Hamilton exposes how his dupes' own naivety,
snobbery or greed make them perfect targets. These three
novels are shot through with the brooding menace and sense
of bleak inevitability so characteristic of the author. There is
also vivid satire and caustic humour. Gorse is thought to be
based on the real-life Neville Heath, hanged in 1946.

'The entertainment value of this brilliantly told story
could hardly be higher' – LP Hartley

Black Spring Press
£9.95 paperback original
ISBN 978-0-948238-34-5
www.blackspringpress.co.uk

LONDON BOOKS RECOMMENDS

THE LIFE OF A LONG-DISTANCE WRITER
The Biography Of Alan Sillitoe

RICHARD BRADFORD

Published to coincide with Alan Sillitoe's 80th birthday in 2008, this is the authorized biography of one of England's most celebrated writers. His first two novels, *Saturday Night And Sunday Morning* and *The Loneliness Of The Long-Distance Runner*, are landmarks in 20th-century fiction and central to the wider cultural phenomenon of the 1950s and 1960s that came to be known as 'kitchen sink'.

Born in Nottingham in 1928, Sillitoe left school with no qualifications. After a series of factory jobs he had a spell in the RAF, during which time he contracted TB and nearly died. While convalescing he began writing, developing the gritty, urban style that made him, for a time, pre-eminent among English novelists. Though he has never replicated the staggering success of those early novels, he has continued to write a book nearly every year since the early 1960s.

Richard Bradford has benefitted from Sillitoe's close co-operation and access to his substantial archive, including never-before-published photographs and correspondence with all of the kitchen-sink luminaries as well as Sillitoe's close friend, Poet Laureate Ted Hughes. *The Life Of A Long-Distance Writer* is sure to be seen as the definitive work on one of the truly great English writers of the 20th century.

Peter Owen Publishers
£25 hardback
ISBN 978-0-7206-1317-x
www.peterowen.com

LONDON BOOKS RECOMMENDS

SATURDAY NIGHT AND SUNDAY MORNING

ALAN SILLITOE

To coincide with Alan Sillitoe's 8oth birthday and the 50th anniversary of its original publication Harper Perennial is reissuing one of the defining novels of the 1950s, *Saturday Night And Sunday Morning*. This edition includes a new introduction by Richard Bradford, author of the Sillitoe biography *The Life Of A Long-Distance Writer*.

The novel is based in working-class Nottingham, where Sillitoe grew up and worked in factory jobs until joining the RAF. It follows the controversial protagonist Arthur Seaton, whose work all day at a lathe in the bicycle factory leaves him with energy to spare in the evenings. A hard-drinking, hard-fighting young rebel, he knows what he wants, and he's sharp enough to get it. Before long, his carryings-on with a couple of married women is local gossip. But then one evening he meets a young girl in a pub, and Arthur's life begins to look less simple . . . Published to instant critical acclaim *Saturday Night And Sunday Morning* is a story of timeless significance and established Sillitoe as one of the greatest British writers of his generation. The film of the novel, starring Albert Finney, transformed British cinema and was much imitated.

Praise for *Saturday Night And Sunday Morning*
'That rarest of all finds: a genuine no-punches-pulled, unromanticised working-class novel. Mr Sillitoe is a born writer, who knows his milieu and describes it with vivid, loving precision.' *Daily Telegraph*

'His writing has real experience in it and an instinctive accuracy that never loses its touch. His book has a glow about it as though he had plugged it into some basic source of the working-class spirit.' *Guardian*

'Miles nearer the real thing than DH Lawrence's mystic, brooding working-men ever came.' *Sunday Express*

Harper Perennial
£7.99 paperback
ISBN 978-0-007205-02-8